CHRISTMAS TRAVESTIES

Also by Alexandria Blaelock

SHORT STORY COLLECTIONS
The Haunting of Hayward Hall
Lovelorn, Lovestruck and Love at First Sight
Common or Garden Variety Heroes
Case Files of the Wilkinson National Detective Agency
Unavoidable Fates

FICTION
That Love Nonsense

MS BLAELOCK'S BOOKS
Stress Free Dinner Parties
Signature Wardrobe Planning
Holistic Personal Finance
Minimally Viable Housekeeping
Planning a Life Worth Living

A SELECTION OF AVAILABLE
SHORT STORIES
Alma's Grace
Balancing the Book
Bygone Boyfriend
Fate in Your Hands
Kiss of Death
Lady of the Looking Glass
Life in the Security Directorate
Love in the Security Directorate
Morning Star, Evening Star, Superstar
Needy Bitch
Payton's Run
Secret Singer
Shining Star
Ship in a Bottle

CHRISTMAS TRAVESTIES

ALEXANDRIA BLAELOCK

BlueMere Books
MELBOURNE, AUSTRALIA

For permission requests, please contact enquiries@bluemerebooks.com.

Ordering Information:
Discounts are available on quantity purchases. For details, contact orders@bluemerebooks.com.

Christmas Travesties/Alexandria Blaelock
hardback ISBN: 978-1-925749-90-8
paperback ISBN: 978-1-925749-91-5
digital ISBN: 978-1-925749-92-2

Book Layout © BookDesignTemplates.co

Contents

INTRODUCTION

I am envious of people who love Christmas, with the purest and simplest of joys.

The ones who lovingly wrap and unwrap their glass decorations from year to year.

The death-defying ones who climb on the roof to string up Christmas lights, (that cost them a fortune in electricity).

And especially the ones who are delighted with gifts of socks, ties and sensible underpants.

Not forgetting the ones who happily wear Christmas jumpers, ties, socks and jewellery. Especially the kind with flashing lights.

And bells.

Christmas and I have had an uneasy relationship for most of my life. Looking back, it seems as though every traumatic event has happened in the lead up to Christmas.

Starting with emigrating to Australia when I was five.

Followed by my parents splitting up, my divorce, my father's death, then my favourite Aunt Muriel's, and not much later, my mother's.

Did you know the lead up to Christmas is also the peak period for transplants?

My transplant came during that period too, and while I am deeply grateful to the family that permitted it, I am very much aware that my life continues through someone else's death.

Mind you, when I was younger, I looked forward to the lead up to Christmas, but not so much to the actual day.

My mother made Christmas puddings in September. Every year until she gave it up when I was about fifteen because she said they didn't cure right.

We'd get out the nasty plastic tree on December 1, (no smell of pine or fallen needles that needed clearing up for us) and pull out the decorations. Some of them survived the trip from England with us. And then we'd fill up the tree and lounge room with them.

Sometime in December Muriel's gifts would arrive from England, always exactly right, with a big tin of Quality Street chocolates and another of

Huntley & Palmer biscuits for the family, right up until the company shut down.

We were allowed one fancy and one plain with our tea, because otherwise we'd scoff all the chocolate ones. My favourite was the bon bon.

And on Christmas Eve the gifts would appear under the tree, and "Santa" came by after we were asleep.

Always with a stocking made from a football sock that included an orange in the heel, and a string bag of unshelled nuts in the toe.

But Christmas Day itself was almost invariably a nightmare.

Dad would get drunk, my parents would fight, and my brother and I would disappear until tea time so we didn't have to see it.

Year after year, the same pattern.

Even after they split up.

There's something insane about a family Christmas when there's no family.

One year, when I was about twenty-five, we had Christmas at mine. I don't remember the exact details, but Dad got drunk and accused Mum of ruining Christmas.

It's become a kind of code for me and my husband, a sly tongue-in-cheek dig for things of no consequence.

Bad haircut? "He ruined Christmas." Shop ran out of milk? "They ruined Christmas." Doctor's running late? "She ruined Christmas."

I can't be the only one that feels this way.

So I decided to put my own collection of stories together for Christmas, and just like those tins of biscuits, or boxes of chocolate, this collection includes something bitter and sweet. Dark, nutty and plain.

Starting with *Christmas Bonanza*; it takes beauty, brains and brawn to win The Christmas Bonanza - the most anticipated reality show on TV. But Edina Montrose wants to win. No matter the cost.

Then the *Remains of Christmas*; having spent all her life in the military, all Penelope Cradock knows is how to be a soldier. Never married, lost her unit and her family in the war. And while the Empire conquered her people, Christmas conquered the Empire.

In *Christmas Kisses* Ava Gibson, slightly stressed event manager, organising the Goldings Investment Bank annual Christmas dinner. Ryan Griffith, high flyer, confirmed bachelor, and Christmas Sceptic. Knocking heads together. Literally.

And during the *Christmas Conflagration*, Matilda May McDonald, so-called crazy catlady, owner of four dogs, trapped by her past. Perhaps this Christmas offers more than salvation.

Finally, *Christmas Business*, where Vada Paloma was busy working undercover. So deep undercover she can't find her way back. Could Christmas be the key to unlocking her present?

So I hope you...

if not exactly enjoy, then are perhaps satisfied with these stories.

Alexandria Blaelock
Melbourne, Australia
November 2021

CHRISTMAS BONANZA

Edina Montrose was nervous.

It was September first; the day *The Christmas Bonanza* competition began.

It was the ultimate reality show; beauty, brains, and brawn. Open to men and women sixteen to twenty-six.

And of course, the ultimate winner deserves the ultimate prize.

The magnificent house and gardens were constructed and furnished by the competitors. Brand new cars and clothes supplied by the sponsors.

And of course - a marriage made in heaven, between the two fittest, smartest, most beautiful people in the country.

With all that, it was no wonder *The Christmas Bonanza* was the most anticipated reality show on TV.

Competitors were voted off, back on, and off again by competitors and audience alike.

Challenges included hunting game and preparing one or more meals for the other competitors.

Plus quizzes, talent shows, and survival skills.

Winner takes all.

Edina sat on a Queen Anne style stool, facing herself in the triple mirrors of the dressing table, wondering if she was doing the right thing.

She picked up a photo of her family; Mum, Dad, four sisters and herself, the youngest.

She was young when it was taken, and it had seemed to her that anything was possible.

She was older now.

Cynical too.

Believed you had to work harder, not smarter, to get anywhere in life.

Was she was too old to win *The Christmas Bonanza?*

Too saggy, and bumpy, and daggy?

Too dumb?

It was worth it, right?

She desperately wanted to prove herself.

To her family, and to everyone who said she'd never amount to anything.

And this year was the last year she was eligible to enter; born on December 24th, she'd age out near the end of the competition.

Edina had resolved that this year, no matter the cost, she would do *whatever* it took.

She looked past herself, to the reflection of the room behind him.

The blue sponged walls looked like a warm summer sky. Deep blue wall-to-wall carpet, made you feel like you were lying on a tiny island in the middle of the Mediterranean as you lay in bed.

The Queen Anne bed, wardrobe, side and dressing tables she'd lovingly sanded back to the original birch and applied a clear stain.

The lacework doilies she'd made by hand to protect the furniture from her antique finds.

The watercolour beach landscapes she'd painted and hung in white frames.

And the lush green indoor plants she threw away as soon as they got too big for the room.

On the whole, it presented a charming picture, one she was proud to leave the curtains open for passers-by to see just how beautiful it was.

Not a speck of dirt, or unplumped pillow, or carelessly thrown garment to mar its perfection.

That morning, however, the vine print curtains were closed.

She'd worked her butt off to prepare for the competition.

Training hard, she'd finally lost her puppy fat and built muscle. Her running times were the best they'd ever been.

She'd joined an academy, brushing up her education, and picking *ikebana* for her special knowledge.

Taken piano lessons, practised faithfully until she could play a wide range of classical pieces, and popular music for others to sing along to.

And she'd gone to modelling classes, learning the latest techniques for hair and make-up, how to stand and pose attractively, as well as how to interview and answer the faux-personal questions during her video confessionals.

Even rehearsed the likely screening questions until they were second nature, it was all right there in her head; she was as prepared as she could be.

She'd invested in waxing and a spray tan, a manicure and pedicure, even taken iontophoresis treatments to manage the nervous sweating for the duration of the contest.

That morning she'd done her hair and make-up and dressed in a neat, smooth black satin dress with just a hint of shine.

Her bag was packed with a swimsuit, a simple evening gown, and lightweight body armour.

Edina was as ready as she was ever going to be.

She smoothed the skirt of her dress down the length of a thigh.

Three months without the comfort and support of her family, and that room were difficult to contemplate.

She took a deep breath and stood up.

It was time to leave.

Against her wishes, her family and friends were waiting in the lounge to say goodbye.

No one had said anything, but she felt her lips tremble, and tears gathering in her eyes.

"I wish you reconsider," her mother said.

She smiled a little, "I've worked too hard to get here."

"But hundreds of women from around the country will be there," her father said, "you'll never make it to the final ten."

"I have to try," she replied.

"I'm going to miss you so much," her best friend Sean said.

"Me too," and brushing a tear from her cheek, she dropped her bag and rushed across the room to hug him tightly.

"I have to go," she said, "before I start balling."

"Let me take you," he said.

Outside a car horn tooted, and she shook her head, "my taxi's here."

She hugged them all and left before they could try to change her mind again.

The crowd of people entering through the women's entrance of *The Christmas Bonanza* auditions at the hall was immense.

And when she saw the first of several crews filming the masses, she almost changed her mind and walked away.

Then she remembered what was at stake - she was here to prove herself. She was not going to let a mere billion women take it away.

Edina, you just have to take it minute by minute, she told herself, and squaring her shoulders, joined the sign in throng.

Getting signed in seemed the first challenge.

A long queue snaked down a series of corridors like a labyrinth.

She looked around while she waited, and noticed several cameras fixed to the walls and ceiling and nodded. Of course, it would be impossible to use a film crew in this crush. A sensible precaution.

She counted them as she went, and wondered if they were using facial recognition.

When she finally reached the head of the queue, she was waved through to one of several counters.

When she got to the counter, the young woman wearing a *The Christmas Bonanza* t-shirt behind it flipped through an enormous book and crossed her name off, and took a quick headshot.

Then printed it onto a luggage tag, fixed it to Edina's bag and dropped it on the conveyor belt behind her, saying, "your bag will be delivered to your destination."

Then she printed a name tag, an entry form, the Release of Liability waiver, and a sheaf of papers describing the competition terms and conditions.

Edina noted a camera fixed in such a way it was looking directly at her, and did not kid herself this was anything other than the first personality test.

She stood with poise, applied her name tag as soon as it was passed over, and chatted politely while she waited to complete the formalities.

When she was waved through to the next stage, she smiled, bowed a little, and thanked the woman for her time.

The first thing she saw was as she entered the next room was another camera, and then a woman in a black suit. She gave Edina a brief explanation of the terms, paying particular attention to the Release of Liability.

In this instance, the camera was probably for due diligence, but she had no idea who was watching.

She sat elegantly, asked intelligent questions about the details, and politely thanked the woman as she witnessed her signature on the forms.

She waved Edina through another door, where she joined another camera surveilled queue and was directed to a room where rows of desks were lined up like an examination hall.

Criss-crossed by camera angles.

A large digital display hanging on the wall at the front was set to 60:00.

When the desks were full, the door closed, and presumably, the queue moved onto the next room.

Several young women in tiny shorts and *The Christmas Bonanza* t-shirts started handing out quiz booklets labelled DO NOT TURN OVER UNTIL INSTRUCTED, along with multiple choice answer sheets 300 questions long and a lead pencil.

Another explained, "we're about to administer the first test, those of you who do not pass will be going home."

She disregarded the sound of anxious voices.

"You have one hour to complete 300 questions. The test is computer-graded, so please carefully colour in the circles."

She also disregarded the sound of someone further down retching.

"Your time starts now," she slapped a button on the desk starting the digital timer, "please turn over your question books."

The initial questions were easy enough, but by 15 minutes in, she was struggling and starting to tense up.

She took a deep breath and held it as she watched the clock tick over ten seconds before letting it out.

She reasoned the level of difficulty of the questions would be random in an attempt to cull the numbers as much as possible.

Therefore, if she skimmed over the questions she couldn't immediately answer, she would answer more overall.

And once she'd gone through, she could go back and try the hard ones again.

She attempted to turn the pages quietly so the competition wouldn't catch what she was doing.

And by the time the clock signalled the end of the session, Edina had not only been proved correct, but felt she'd answered way more questions than otherwise.

She permitted herself to stretch her arms and legs out as the women collected up the books, pencils, and answer sheets.

"Congratulations to you all.

"If you follow the corridor to the end, you'll find the dining hall where we've prepared a delicious lunch for you.

Toilet facilities are located on either side. You will be told where to go when lunch is over."

Chairs scraped on the floor as the competitors leapt to their feet to rush from the room, either to get the free food before it ran out, or the toilets.

Like disembarking plane passengers, clogging the corridor in the process.

Edina stayed seated until the stampede had moved on, then stood and pushed her chair back under the table. She thanked the women as she left the room.

What she really wanted to do, was run around to release some of the tension she'd built up during the test.

But with no mention of the outside, she settled for arm stretches as she walked up the corridor.

Having waited in the room, a toilet was free when she got there.

It was becoming a game as she checked for cameras, but there were none in the bathroom.

And having gone to the toilet first, dining room servers in the same tiny shorts and *The Christmas Bonanza* t-shirts were replenishing the buffet of hot and cold, sweet and savoury food.

She noted six cameras as she considered what the next event might be.

Most likely not napping.

Having just completed a quiz, probably not brain-related. Most likely something physical.

So, what she needed was something to provide a lot of energy, fight fatigue and keep hunger at bay for several hours of intense activity.

Probably not pizza, pasta, or burgers. Or the sugary and alcoholic drinks. Or the cakes and cookies.

Perhaps a piece of grilled chicken, and a baked potato with a light salad. Orange juice to drink. Followed by a banana or pear.

Taking just enough for her needs, to stop eating when she was about 80% full.

A woman in the service area caught her eye, and she smiled and nodded her thanks.

She found an empty seat, said hello to the women who were already there, and listened as they talked amongst themselves.

They clearly already knew each other and didn't think it was worth getting to know her. Mind you, none of them knew who would be progressing to the next stage anyway.

About an hour later, another woman in shorts and a sloganed t-shirt made an announcement.

"You have been placed into groups of 50; the details are posted in the next room. Please note the number of the coach you 've been assigned to, and make your way to the vehicles waiting to take you to the next destination for the next challenge."

Once again, chairs scraped as people rushed to leave. Edina collected her lunch things together, hesitated a moment, then collected together her table mates abandoned dishes, and took them all to the clearly marked return chute.

Once again, she saw a woman behind her counter and she smiled her thanks and nodded.

She took her time, visiting the bathroom, and washing her hands, and when she got to the next room, the crowd had thinned out.

She noted her coach number, and half hoped her lunch uncompanions wouldn't land places in her coach. Or the show for that matter, because sharing a dormitory with those self-absorbed women would probably have been a nightmare.

Then again, she had no idea how many people applied, or how many had to be excluded before they made it to the show.

The first few episodes were usually devoted to narrowing the number of candidates down to 100 men and 100 women, so she supposed the day was all about getting rid of the low hanging fruit.

Was it even possible they might get down to 100 women today?

She didn't see the women from lunch as she boarded the coach, nor did she know anyone.

Not surprising really, she hadn't told anyone she was entering, because she was a little embarrassed about having applied.

She thought she was too old and didn't want to have to explain why.

Too late, she wished she hadn't written it in the application. That she was afraid of being alone for the rest of her life. That she was bored and wanted to meet new people.

But she supposed someone was already using it to prepare the marketing information about her.

And someone else was using it to script encounters she might have with her competitors.

The city scenery made way for the suburbs, and after about half an hour, the coach pulled up at a sports stadium.

Looked like her surmise was correct; an afternoon of sporting events.

A woman in the ubiquitous shorts and t-shirt stood up to make an announcement, Edina thought she recognised her from the morning's testing.

This time she explained the afternoon's events.

"Congratulations on progressing to the next stage. This afternoon is all about Athletics.

"You can choose any one of five events to compete in. The events are Discus, High Jump, Long Jump, Shot Put, and 400m Sprints.

"When you exit the bus, please follow the guides into the stadium. We've provided sports clothes and shoes, so check the tables on your way in.

"As you enter the stadium, you'll see signs for the events; please assemble at the appropriate sign.

"Good luck with your chosen event."

And with that, she left the coach and walked through the entry of the stadium.

As Edina changed into the same skimpy shorts and *The Christmas Bonanza* t-shirt as the crew and assistants were wearing, Edith was a little uncomfortable. She wouldn't usually wear anything that tight or brief.

She packed her black dress and shoes in the bag the sports gear came in, and affixed the name sticker she'd been issued with to it.

Edina decided to do the sprint. She was more of a 100m sprinter, but it's not like there were likely to be any professional runners in the competition.

This time, film crews were allocated to each sport, and because they were in a professional venue, there were overhead cameras suspended on wires across the stadium.

The sprints started with the usual basic competition; eight girls running the track, those who placed, rested and waited for the next race.

Those who didn't were escorted from the field.

The months spent running had served Edina well. She paced herself and came in the top three every race until the last.

Edina, she told herself, *you've already made it, you have nothing to prove. But just for fun, why not try to win this time?*

She smiled and thought why not?

So she put her game face on and ran as fast as she could, and was a little surprised when she won.

Even more surprised when they presented bronze, gold, and silver medals to the finalists of each event, in front of the crowd of competitors.

Was that a way to make early enemies?

The origianl t-shirted woman made another announcement, "Congratulations to the winners, and to you all.

"We've prepared an evening meal for you.

"But first you will be escorted to the change rooms where you can shower. Once more there are packs of clothes, shoes and toiletries to change into, so check in at the tables on your way in to claim your size.

"Your groups of fifty have been redistributed for the next leg; the details will be posted as you exit the change rooms.

"Please note your coach number, and look for the signs when you make your exit.

"You have thirty minutes to get ready."

Which triggered a rush to the clothing table.

Edina turned to congratulate her fellow finalists, "congratulations on your medal," she said, holding out her hand.

The silver medallist frowned, "do you think there'll be hair-dryers?"

"Probably not with only thirty minutes to prepare," Edina said.

"Shame, my hair frizzes when it's wet," said Bronze.

"Would you like to borrow my hair elastic to pull it back into a bun?" Edina asked.

"Actually, that would be great."

Edina pulled it off, dragged a few stray hairs from it, and handed it over.

"I have some bobby pins," silver offered.

Bronze smiled, "thank you. "My name's Joanna by the way."

"Bethany," said silver.

"Edina, pleased to meet you." She indicated the table where the crowd was thinning out, "shall we?"

They sauntered over, and Edina gestured for them to go first.

When Edina got to the table, they were out of her size, a size larger, and the size larger than that.

She smiled and shrugged, "can't be helped. I'll manage something," and taking the package, she followed what was left of the crowd to the shower room.

At least the shoes fit; white ballet style pumps with an elasticated type of fabric upper.

The dress was a plain, A-line white shift, with nothing to distinguish itself.

She hung it up and thought about her options while she was showered.

Was there anything she could use as a belt? Or a safety pin to fold it around her body in a faux-wrap dress? Or tie a knot in it?

She slathered on the generic moisturiser, put on the surprisingly stretchy undies, and abandoned the bra.

There was no make-up included, which she imagined would terrify some of the other competitors.

Luckily, she was one of the last in the room, and scouting around, found a couple of safety pins and an abandoned thin, blue ribbon on the floor. She towelled the ribbon dry, and hung it on a hook while she prepare to dress.

First she pinned up the dress's armholes. The slipped it on, folded the excess material across her front, and then tied the ribbon around her body, under her bust to hold the folds in place.

Not the best, not the worst, but it'd have to do.

She hurried out to meet the coach.

On the way, she wondered why everyone was wearing the same thing.

Her first thought was some kind of creepy virgin sacrifice, but the news had been covering the build-up to the competition.

Then she imagined the potentially amusing explanation of the mass slaughter to the police.

Which had never been the subject of news coverage in previous years.

And then more realistically, that they would be judging the female form.

Without any fancy clothes, make-up or elaborate hairstyles to distract them, they would be able to see the "real" girl.

Dusk was drawing in when they arrived at their destination; a large, Renaissance Revival style mansion with a large tower positioned between two symmetrical wings.

Their destination was a large reception room on the ground floor of the tower. It had wooden floors and high ceilings of elaborately moulded and painted plaster.

That there were cameras in the corners came as no real surprise.

Large archways led to other rooms, presumably one of them being a dining room.

A grand piano sat in one corner, the stool slightly pulled out, as if the pianist had just nipped out for a quick ciggy.

At least three film crews were in attendance, and t-shirted people walked around offering half-full champagne glasses.

Edina was starting to get a little tired of seeing *The Christmas Bonanza* logo.

The women wearing the t-shirts all looked the same; same tiny shorts, the canvas sneakers, same sleek ponytails.

And seeing as they weren't offering anything else to drink, she took a glass of champagne, idly wondering how many women were in the room.

She looked around, trying to guess, and realised there weren't any men.

And considering further, she hadn't seen any men at any point since she'd walked into the audition that morning.

Not entirely sure why that struck her as odd, as if they were a large harem attended only by women.

It could just be a little something extra for the female competitor's comfort, but given the supposed cut-throat nature of the competition, it seemed counter to the spirit.

She sipped her champagne, and noticing Bethany in the crowd, sent her a toast. She smiled and walked over.

"It's really quite beautiful here, isn't it?" she said.

Edina grunted agreement, "but all those Christmas Bonanza women are kinda creeping me out."

"Are they?" Bethany looked around her. "Now that I'm looking, they are kind of... I don't know, plasticky?" She took a sip of her champagne, "oh look, there's Joanna."

Bethany waved a hand to attract Joanna's attention; her face brightened as she recognised them, and she walked across the room to them.

"Hello again," she said, smoothing back her hair, "thanks again for the elastic and hairpins - you're lifesavers."

Edina smiled and nodded, Bethany said, "you're welcome."

"Is it just me, or is there something about this place that strikes you as a bit odd?" Joanna asked.

"Edina was just saying about the women from the show."

"What about them?" Joanna looked at Edina

But she was looking at one in particular, "I could have sworn that was one of the women who shared my lunch table, but why would she be serving here?"

Bethany and Joanna turned to watch as Edina approached the woman.

"Hello," she said to the woman, who attempted to brush past her, but Edina blocked her path, "Hello again."

The woman looked at her with no sign of recognition, and Edina took a step back, eyes widening.

"What happened?" Bethany asked.

"There's no one there; her eyes are dead inside."

Bethany and Joanna exchanged a look.

"Okay then. We need to find someone else we know to check," Bethany said, and they looked areound the room.

"Hold up," said Joanna, and approached another woman while Bethany and Edina watched.

Not long later she was back, "I knew her in high school, but she barely looked at me, and when I refused another glass, she just walked away!"

"Third time's the charm," Bethany said, crossing to another woman.

Then coming back, "I think we can safely say something is very wrong here."

They nodded, and Joanna asked, "but what?"

Edina rubbed her temple with one hand, then took a sip of her drink. "Is it possible the screening is not to get into the show, but whether you have the right kind of disposition to get sidelined into some other kind of activity?"

"Like a cult or something?" asked Bethany.

Joanna nodded, "I read something in the news about how runaways always spike this time of year, and no one knows why."

"No one would think to link it to *The Christmas Bonanza* auditions would they?" Bethany shivered.

Edina slapped her forehead, "and like big numpties, we walked in here willingly, leaving our friends and family thinking we'd be gone for three months, and all our worldly goods in the care of whoever these people are."

"I can't believe I did that. Not to mention signing the non-disclosure agreement and liability waivers," Joanna said.

Bethany drummed her fingers on a thigh, "so, do we bail right now, or wait for... I don't know what."

"I feel like now might be best," Edina said, "before they herd us back into the coaches to go to wherever our next destination is. Then again, this place is like a gussied-up prison, so it could well be the last stop."

"But how?" Joanna took a large gulp of her drink, "it's not like we can just walk out of here. And in any case, we have no idea where we are."

"Perhaps we should try to find a phone to call the police?" said Bethany.

"I was going to say, let's give ourselves an hour to find a phone and then go, but we don't have any way to tell the time either." Edina was starting to feel defeated.

They looked at each other miserably.

Edina stamped her foot. "I came here determined to win this bloody thing, and now they've changed the rules. I am not going to lose to them.

"I don't think we can rely on anyone or anything except ourselves. We have to get out of this place, and the sooner the better. And if I have to walk/run, then I'm going to do just that."

The others looked at her doubtfully.

"I'm scared," Bethany said, and Joanna nodded.

"I understand. I don't know if I'm overreacting, and I don't know if I'm going to make it. But this time, I'm going to trust—"

They heard a crash as someone dropped a glass, and turned to look.

One of the younger competitors had dropped her glass and fainted.

"Just a little too much to drink," one of the show women said, as another couple of women clustered around her to help lift her up and carry her away.

Edina, Bethany and Joanna looked at each other and found places to leave their half-empty glasses.

As one they turned and started walking towards the entrance.

A show woman intercepted them, "where are you going?"

"Oh," said Edina, "just need the bathroom."

The woman looked suspicious, but directed them, "to your left as you go down the corridor."

"Thank you so much," said Bethany.

Joanna offered a bright smile, "lovely party."

Together they walked in the indicated direction, conscious of the woman looking after them.

"That was close," Joanna giggled nervously, "but I really do have to go now."

Edina splashed cold water on her face, then used the toilet.

Bathroom break taken care of, Edina opened the door a crack, "doesn't seem to be anyone watching," she whispered, "let's check any vehicles we see, and if we can't use them, we'll run for it, okay?"

The others nodded.

They managed to sneak out without anyone catching them.

Though with the number of cameras about, Edina couldn't be certain.

Crouching low, she ran to the first car she saw and tried the door.

It was locked! She ran on to the next.

Bethany ran to another, and got the door open, but couldn't find a key.

Joanna whistled, and having got their attention, she beckoned them over. The girls, crouching low, ran to the car and climbed inside.

"Fingers crossed," Joanna said, and turned the key.

It caught, and she gunned it, spraying gravel as she fishtailed up the long drive.

"Left or right?" she asked as she got to the end.

"Right," said Edina, the coach turned left to get into the place.

They drove for a few minutes, "wait, isn't this the Princess Freeway?" asked Bethany.

"I dunno, is it?" Joanna said, "and are we going in the right direction?"

They looked out into the darkness trying to tell.

"Hold up," Edina shouted, and Joanna slammed on the brakes, "I think we just passed a police sign."

Joanna grunted, "probably be repeated closer to the next junction," but she drove at something more closely approximating the speed limit.

After a few more kilometres, they followed the police signs through smaller and smaller streets until they reached the building.

Joanna pulled over and parked the car; "I have to admit I feel a little silly right now," she said.

"Me too," admitted Bethany.

"Me three," said Edina, "but if there's the smallest chance I'm right about the situation, I have to say something."

She got out of the car, and the others followed her into the police station.

And sat with her as she explained her gut feeling to a stony-faced detective.

Who said nothing for the longest time as he looked at her.

And then sighed.

"I'll send a car to investigate. In the meantime, you can call someone to come get you.

The scandal broke not long after.

That the Eternal Light Movement had created *The Christmas Bonanza* as a recruitment drive.

That almost all the competitors were brain-washed and sent away as slave labour within the first week.

That the footage of the first week was cut and pasted together into enough different episodes to last the full three months of programmed episodes.

That many of the sponsors had ties to the movement and benefited from the labourers.

That deprogrammers had been called in.

The tax office was investigating, along with other State and national regulatory bodies.

That three plucky competitors had been suspicious and led to the investigation that brought the movement down.

Closer to Christmas, Edina met up with Joanna and Bethany at a wine bar in the city.

They were shown to a booth, ordered some snacks and cocktails while they decided what to eat.

"I like how reassuringly normal this place is," commented Joanna.

"Oh yes," Bethany agreed.

Edina raised her glass, "to normality," and the others chinked glasses with her.

Bethany laid a hand on Edina's arm, "we had a lucky escape thanks to you."

Edina shrugged, "we did it together."

"I doubt I would've had the courage on my own," Joanna said.

Edina sipped her drink, "we were lucky; I shudder to think what might have happened."

"So what's next?" asked Bethany, "I've got a new job."

Joanna grinned, "Nice one! I've applied to go to University."

They looked at Edina.

"I don't know. I'd pinned all my hopes on winning the competition for some kind of direction, and now that's gone. I think I need some time to grieve and let it go."

Bethany smoothed a lock of hair back behind her ears, "I understand, but don't take too long."

"Uh-huh," said Joanna, "think about the skills you didn't know you had. The ones that helped you see something wasn't quite right about the show.

"Why not put them to good use, like a journalist, perhaps the police force, or one of the agencies?"

Edina grunted, and speared some fried halloumi, "not sure I'd want to be in front of it again, but I could do some kind of analysis I guess."

She brightened, "something to think about anyway."

She raised her glass again, "here's to a Merry Christmas, and an uneventful New Year."

Bethany raised her glass, "Merry Christmas."

"Definitely an uneventful New Year," agreed Joanna.

THE END

REMAINS OF CHRISTMAS

I loved Christmas when I was young, for as far back as I can remember.

When I was a child, it was all about Dad.

He was in service, but rather than following him from base to base like other military families, Mother insisted the rest of us stay in one place.

"I want to live like a normal family," she declared.

And so, the rest of us did.

But then I suppose, hers was a farming family, not military. Her roots were buried deep in the soil for a hundred generations.

Such a stereotype to fall in love with a boy from the base, especially as she'd made it a rule to avoid them.

Though having seen pictures of him when he was younger, I can understand that.

I would have gone for him too, straight and true as an arrow.

Mother had pinned her hopes on marrying a farmer from one of the neighbouring towns, and by the time she realised Dad was from the base, not another town, it was too late.

She was sweet on him.

It's another cliché that the heart wants what the heart wants, but it was certainly true for her.

Dad moved from base to base as the years passed, but without fail, he came home in mid-December and stayed for four weeks before shipping out again.

And every time he left she was pregnant again.

I thought an annual baby was normal.

When I was older, I heard a joke about a couple having sex once a year and suddenly it clicked - it wasn't just that Mother was very good at catching the stork's attention as it flew over.

I guess no one bothered with that joke about our family, because her annual cycle was so obvious.

So in anticipation, our preparations for Christmas usually started late September with getting the Christmas puddings ready.

For weeks our house would smell of dried fruits steeping in brandy, and then a little later, as the puddings were mixed and cooked, of cinnamon, cloves and sweet treacly cooked sugar.

Later still, they'd sit in the larder, gently perfuming the air as they intensified in flavour.

Makes my mouth water just thinking about it, though I've never made a pudding myself.

I suppose pudding making is a lost domestic art, though perhaps someone somewhere continues the tradition.

As September gave way to October, the attention focused on preparing the house for Dad's arrival.

Unlike other women who leave the household maintenance to their husbands, Mother wanted to gift him the opportunity to fully relax at home.

And presumably take care of her.

Ahem.

So, during October and November, she started going through the house room by room; sweeping, cleaning and painting.

We'd come home from school, never knowing when it was our room's turn and we'd have to sleep on a pile of blankets on the floor.

I can't imagine what a winter Christmas would be like, but thank goodness ours falls over Summer and we could leave the windows open to let the smell of fresh paint out.

And cook outside to prevent the smell settling into the clean house.

As November gave way to December, we would reach fever pitch.

The paint would be clean and dry. The house spic and span. And we would be fully occupied with cleaning the old Christmas decorations and making the new while Mother made stacks of shortbread, gingerbread biscuits, and fruit mince pies.

We'd make huge strings of popcorn, though I still don't understand the purpose of them. Aside from tasks to keep us occupied during the school holidays, and snacks for times when our parents had "things" to do.

And then chains made from slips of paper glued end-to-end.

Scavenging pine cones from around the farm and painting them white, silver and gold.

Sticks bent into star shapes and wrapped with twine. Weaving scraps of fabric into heart shapes.

And then one day, out of the blue, Gunnery Sergeant Philip James Craddock would come walking up the long farm drive, blue uniform jacket hanging open, with his duffel bag slung over his shoulder.

When it was my turn, I realised she always knew when he was coming, because Aunty Allison who owned the town beauty salon would visit the house that morning.

But for us, it was on.

Racing down the drive to be the first to meet him, and be folded into his enormous hug.

I don't know how Mother could stand on the porch waiting for him.

Perhaps the knowledge the night was hers helped. And with that in mind, they did their very best to exhaust us so we went to bed early.

The next day, was the only day of the year Mother could sleep in.

Or perhaps *wanted* to sleep in.

Dad would creep out of bed early and cook us a "military" breakfast of sausage, beans and eggs.

And then he'd take us all out across the farm looking for the best Christmas tree.

Even the baby.

And he would keep us out all day, stopping for a picnic lunch of sandwiches and homemade orange cordial he'd prepared earlier.

Exhausted, happy and triumphant, we'd come home late in the day to put the tree up and decorate it, along with the house.

And that evening, after dinner, we'd sit outside on the verandah and eat the first of the Christmas puddings, with rich creamy custard.

Somehow Dad would always get the threepenny bit, and he would look at his children ranged around him with pride, and flick it into the air above us.

And somehow, it would always be me that caught it.

Looking back, those days were truly magical.

The sun was always shining, the days were always balmy and warm, and mosquitoes never bit.

But isn't childhood always glorious when you look back?

Then one year, Dad didn't come walking up the drive.

Two officers, a man and a woman, arrived in a staff car instead.

They took their hats off when they saw Mother standing on the verandah.

Something strange was going on, and we clustered restlessly together nearby to watch.

They saluted her at the foot of the stairs, with a smart, precisely timed swing of their arms. Then walked up to the house and offered her an envelope. Something was said, and she nodded.

They walked back down the stairs, turned back to face her, offering another salute before they climbed into the car and drove away.

It seemed to me they sought me out among the bunch of us.

I was watching them so intently I didn't see her fall, nor the rest of my siblings flock to her side.

It took my eldest brother several shouts to attract my attention and send me running helter-skelter through the wheat fields for Grandmother.

Shortly after that, it was no real surprise to anyone in my extended family that I announced my intention to attend the Military Academy.

I had not been able to shake the memory of those officers, driving that car, saluting Mother in their deepest of deep blue uniforms topped with the striking silver braiding.

The neat efficiency and synchronicity of their movements.

The perfect precision of their haircuts.

More importantly, their sleek, well-fed bodies.

As we stood on the train station, the train huffing and puffing in its eagerness to leave, Mother hugged me tightly and said, "I wish it wasn't you of all my children."

My eldest brother said she stood waving, long after the train had disappeared from sight.

But I had left the farm without looking back.

For me, life was just beginning, and I was looking forward to it.

I remember the day I arrived at the Academy, its grey stone walls looming above me. Some say it looks more like a prison, but I loved the way its tall brutal buildings assaulted the sky.

I loved its lush green sports ovals and parade grounds, the formal gravel drives and pathways leading directly from one building to another, and the way it was built into the cliffs surrounding it.

Manifestly defensible.

But even more than that, I loved the statue of the mounted hussar in the main forecourt.

Leaning forward, sword drawn, charging towards the main gate as though challenging each and every person to sought entry.

As if it knew who was worthy and who was not.

I cannot have been the only one who stood taller and straighter in the face of his challenge.

I remember meeting the Recruit Sergeant the first time, and the height his eyebrows achieved when I loudly announced myself "Cadet Penelope June Craddock, reporting for duty."

He almost took a step back to get a better look at me. Something I noticed as I met each of the Officers who undertook student training.

And for a short time after graduating into the forces.

And the reason for this was that Dad had been an Academy legend in his time.

Top of every single class.

Decent margins between him and the next in Military Strategy and Military History.

Time trial wins on the cross-country runs up the mountain, and down to the bay.

And Captain of the winning team in the final battle simulation.

It was a lot to live up to, but I made up my mind I was going to beat every single one of his records.

I wanted to win against everyone, and graduate as the most successful candidate ever.

Of course, it was hard having grown up on a farm instead of a base.

But I pursued my goal with intense focus; accompanied by no one, excepting a photo of Dad I'd carefully cut out of an old yearbook in the library with my hideously sharp penknife.

While the other kids were meeting up and getting drunk on the top of the administration building, I was in the wilds, running like there was no tomorrow.

And when they were getting drunk down on the beach hidden by a fold in the cliffs, I was practising drills on my own.

And when they were getting drunk up on the mountain in a disused powder magazine, I was studying in my room.

Christmas that first year, I had written to my eldest brother, telling him when I would arrive, and asking him to keep it a secret from Mother.

I walked from the train station, and up the long farm drive, grey cadet uniform hanging open, with my duffel bag slung over my shoulder.

It felt to me as though Dad's spirit had been lost, found me at the Academy, and followed me home.

Neither Mother nor my siblings had any idea I was coming.

Except the eldest of course, and he had somehow got them all in the yard doing stuff as I approached.

It was so wonderful to see them; as if I'd picked up my longing for home and family at the gate where I'd left it on my way out.

I could see them milling about, in confusion, not knowing who I was.

Mother figured it out first, and as she ran lightly down the steps and out onto the drive, she picked up speed.

I dropped my duffel and braced myself as she ran into my hug.

And after a moment, the smallest children who barely remembered me after a year's absence ran after Mother, and gradually the elder siblings figured it out and proceeded toward me at a more leisurely pace.

Until I was in the centre of a rugby scrum of hugging.

Even after my siblings let go and moved back, Mother remained clinging like a barnacle.

I didn't mean to take over Dad's role at Christmas; it was just that my internal clock had moved to Morning Watch while I was at the Academy - I'd needed the extra hours to study.

So as I got up and tip-toed to the kitchen to make myself coffee, planning to go out into the farm until everyone else was awake, my siblings joined me one by one.

Expecting what they thought was a typical "military" breakfast of sausage, beans and eggs.

But which I knew by then was all that Dad could cook.

I didn't want to disappoint them, so I made breakfast. Only *I* left a plate wrapped in foil on a very low heat in the oven for Mother, and made my siblings wash the dishes and clean up the kitchen.

While they did that, I got the youngest up, and left a note propped on the coffee pot to let Mother know the kids were fine with me and hadn't been kidnapped.

And we went out to do what we had always done, venture out across the farm to find the best Christmas tree.

One of the others had prepared sandwiches and homemade orange cordial, so the whole flock of us stayed out all day.

Returning exhausted, happy and triumphant, to put the tree up and decorate it, along with the house.

Regardless of whatever else Mother thought about me taking the siblings out, she prepared the last of the year before's Christmas puddings.

And after dinner, we sat on the verandah and ate it with rich creamy custard.

My eldest brother tucked a bright, shiny three-penny bit into my hand. I looked around at Mother and my siblings, then flicked it into the air above them.

As if time had slowed down, it spun end-over-end and landed in the skirts of the youngest of them. I glanced at my eldest brother, and he nod-ded, just once, with satisfaction.

And so in this way, the pattern for the next five years of my education were set.

I wish I could say how happy I was to graduate with honours, beating every single one of my class-mates, and Dad's records.

Even if I only made one true friend in all that time.

But the so-called War of Independence broke out, and we cadets were sent out to defend the country without even their qualifying ranks to protect them.

I left without looking back.

Instead of the expected analysis role, my first deployment was in command of a small fighting unit.

I'm not ashamed to say I looked at the well-seasoned fighting men, and I as good as shat my pants at the thought of commanding them.

But I was very fortunate to have under my command, a number of men who'd served with Dad.

And I had the good sense to listen to their experience, and plan my plays according to their strengths.

Somehow, we managed to hold our own until December.

It was Christmas that caught us.

Foolishly I'd allowed a ration of brandy that day, because, well, Christmas. And the pudding.

Because we were all tired, bored, and homesick.

And because I thought we were safe in our foxhole; I didn't set reliable sentries.

But for the Empire, Christmas was just another day.

We were the last unit caught by the Empire, and in that way, I'd built my own reputation on the foundation of Dad's strategic military brilliance.

I thought they'd just shoot us, after all, if I'd been in charge, that's would I have done.

Best strategic outcome.

And in any case, they'd bombed the crap out of the country.

Including my childhood home, and all my relatives, evaporated with half the county as a lesson to the rest of us.

For some, the internment camp was a kind of holiday. Conditions weren't bad, the food was good and regular, and many units relaxed their conduct.

Perhaps they'd been so completely demoralised they didn't care anymore. Or perhaps they'd never comported themselves with military dignity.

All captured military personnel have a duty to escape, so I kept my unit focused on planning and working towards an escape.

And well away from the unruly mob we were quartered with.

One day we were called to an assembly in the main quadrangle. I listened with incredulity as they outlined a kind of lottery granting us freedom.

A few of us at a time, to spend some time in isolation and retraining before being released into the community.

The lotteries took place weekly, twenty at a time.

We'd assemble in the quadrangle. They assured us once again that all our names were in the barrel. Then span it round and round, and drew a name. Span it again, and drew someone else.

Like a game show.

After a couple of weeks, I realised that the draws weren't really random.

The people slated for freedom were all highly skilled individuals whose skills could be put to use elsewhere.

Once they'd been deprogrammed.

I pulled the unit together to add this information to the data we already had.

My own Sergeant was surprised it had taken me that long to connect the dots, but he was always a highly suspicious individual.

Well experienced in more personal fields useful to me, but wouldn't get him a ticket out.

The consensus of the unit, was that *when* they called my name, I should leave without a fight.

In the meantime, we'd continue working on the plan and implement it as soon as possible.

But this wasn't the kind of camp you could escape. We all knew that when the list of names ran out, it would be curtains for those left behind.

That Christmas, my name was drawn.

We'd shared a good meal, with a ration of alcohol before the call. It had gone to my head by the time I hugged each of my men and walked towards the guards.

As the gates closed behind me, I heard gunfire break out behind me.

I'd been expecting it, yet my legs still froze for an instant, and my heart skipped a beat before I walked on.

Not looking back.

Vowing that I would somehow find it within me to live a full and active life on my unit's behalf.

That was the last Christmas I celebrated.

I'm old now, and I've lived under the Empire's rule for more than three-quarters of my life.

But sometimes, I still wish I could go back to that day and die a valiant, if ultimately useless death.

Now and again, when I get drunk and maudlin, I wonder if they were the lucky ones to be spared what came next.

Not that life within the Empire has been awful for me, though I'm greeted as a traitor or collaborator by my countrymen, and treated as a spy or terrorist by citizens of the Empire.

And that's kind of okay, I'm used to not being one thing or the other.

But regardless of what people think of me personally, my skills as a senior strategic analyst guarantee me a certain amount of leeway.

More so now that I am so thoroughly inculcated with Empire language and social mores I can barely understand my own people.

It makes me wonder what else I might have got away with in the time before the invasion.

The Empire is highly technological, with many novel gadgets that seemed to me like magic.

The things you can do with your minds.

I suppose I'd never seen a need for most of them. But after a while, I adapted, and it seemed I couldn't live without them.

I looked back on my life and wondered how I had ever survived its simplicity.

It's not that we were naive or simple-minded, but that we were short-sighted and complacent.

That's what ultimately cost us the freedom to freely and proudly proclaim our country's name.

Pure arrogance.

I can't say I blame the Emperor; we were clearly begging to be taken down a peg or two.

Or at least that's what the history books say.

Perhaps it's easier for our younglings this way.

As my generation dies out, the next will be the pure products of the Empire's social structures and educational systems.

As for me, I somehow managed to catch up with the technology and provide the innovative edge the Empire was looking for.

To learn and adapt, as I always had.

It can be a terrible life for a conquered people.

Some went mad and refused to adapt, maintaining their traditional dress and language.

And some threw themselves into the new ways.

But I didn't really *believe* in either.

As I wear my black and gold braided uniform, I am conscious the Emperor is watching.

I have lived a modest life and not drawn attention to myself.

I've kept my mouth shut, and never, until now, wrote, said, or done anything that might draw unwarranted attention or cause suspicion.

Christmas however, has not.

It's spread its unique magic across the Empire, but the original meaning is mostly lost, gone underground and into hiding.

Now it's a unique marketing opportunity beamed directly into people's brains.

Compelling them to buy thoughtless tokens of affection they don't feel, for people they don't like.

For about a decade, I've chosen to deploy over the last quarter of the year.

Every October first, I report for duty.

As I take the lift and descend into the shielded basement, the advertising fades and disappears, leaving me with a blissfully empty mind.

Free to think my own thoughts and feel my own emotions and physical sensations, not the implanted ones.

Three blissful months, followed by one more of gradually increasing intensity until the advertising is back to full blast on the first of February.

Some young people like you find it hard to adjust to being alone inside your own head, not all of you can take it.

But you must learn to adapt, to fine-tune your focus; your intelligence work depends on your ability to tune into the nuances.

If you can't, or won't adjust, you'll be sent back to the surface.

Perhaps you'll recover your mind when you get there.

Or perhaps you won't.

Perhaps you'll become one of the "zombies", chained together, sweeping paths in the Imperial Gardens, trapped and unable to escape the silence.

Objects of derision.

Forever.

You've done well to get this far.

I will leave you to the next phase of your training; a Watch's worth of the shielding simulation.

As I closed the door on the recruits, I took a deep breath and let it out.

We lost a couple every session, but it was better to weed them out *before* we started training them to do their actual jobs.

I went back to the control room where my new adjutant had the monitors running and recording.

"Do many recruits report you?"

I smiled at him warmly, "only the exceptional ones like you." I didn't tell him it was part of the testing - those who didn't were weeded out by the end of the quarter.

"And is it true you enjoy the adblocker? The privacy of your own thoughts?"

As a person born in the Empire, he'd been implanted as a baby. Had never known anything other than the conditioning.

"My implant was never turned on."

He sucked in a gasp.

"It was enough for the Emperor that I submitted to the surgery."

I didn't need to tell him that the risk of implanting as an adult was very great. If it hadn't worked, *I* would have been one of the brainless working in the Imperial Gardens.

But I was a soldier, and my job was to fight.

It didn't much matter to me who for.

What could I possibly have done if not this?

Perhaps not for the reasons my unit might have expected, but I lived.

I'd gone through *a* surgery, but I wasn't convinced an implant had been installed.

The thing about conditioning your population from birth, is that they don't have an opinion between them. They're just drones.

For the Emperor, the only realistic option for generating new ideas is conquering other nations.

And as the commander of the last unit captured, the potential loss of my strategic mind may have been too high a price for him to countenance.

So, if my adjunct played his cards right, he could well have his turned off in ten or twenty years.

Something only granted to those with potential.

And the thing about Christmas was that it gave the populace a focus it didn't have before.

A sanitised one of course.

Wouldn't want them getting any ideas.

THE END

CHRISTMAS KISSES

Ava Gibson walked across the green marble foyer floor, refusing to look any higher than the floor.

When she reached the edge of the stairs down onto the ballroom floor, she paused, closing her eyes to fully soak up the atmosphere.

The room was more or less silent, with the hum of quiet conversation amongst those decorating the last of the tables.

She heard the odd chink of crockery and cutlery as the last of the covers were laid out.

Clashes as crates of glasses were stacked up out ready to be filled and passed around by tuxedo clad waiters.

The band tuned their guitars and checked the sound.

The room seemed a little warm, but she'd been running around most of the day getting everything organised and set up.

A cool breeze drifted across her tank top clad shoulders as the air-conditioning cranked up a notch, preparing for the influx of hundreds of dinner guests.

The hotel was too posh to let any cooking smells into the function rooms, but just for a moment, she thought perhaps she could smell the perfume of roasting meats.

After a few more seconds savouring the moment, she pointed her face up, out across the room and opened her eyes.

It looked magnificent.

Even if she did say it herself.

Traditional Christmas with an Australian twist.

Huge garlands of red flowering gum twined with strings of fairy lights and white, silver and gold glass baubles were suspended from the ceiling. They criss-crossed the room, and where they met, gold and silver stars hung, swaying slightly in the strengthening air-conditioning.

Bouquets of gum leaves were mixed with gold and silver painted pine cones were tied up string and hung at intervals along the balustrades of the sweeping stair case.

Large round tables for ten surrounded the edges of the rich, dark red wood parquetry dance floor.

They were spread with thick white tablecloths, the place settings marked with a red plate, topped with a white Christmas themed plate and a starched red napkin folded into a swan.

In the centre of each table, a silver platter held a small, brown paper covered pot tied up with hessian string containing a small, decorated Christmas tree.

No candles unfortunately; health and safety wouldn't allow them.

The stage at the rear held a square steel lighting stand, decorated with garlands of large red, green and gold ribbons, also twined with twinkling lights. A large wreath of the same materials was suspended from the top of the frame.

The band left the stage to wait for the first set, and the room's internal PA system started playing the Christmas songs.

It was just perfect.

Goldings Investment Bank was the biggest bank in Melbourne, and if they liked what she'd done, it might even make her reputation.

She let out the breath she hadn't realised she was holding, and started to critically assess each part of the room.

Goldings could just as easily ruin her reputation as make it. Her event management business wasn't established enough to take any of it for granted.

But.

It all looked to be in order.

Ava checked her watch, and decided she just had enough time for a quick shower before she changed into her evening gown and came back to oversee the operation of the evening.

She hadn't seen her boyfriend Max by the time she left the room, though that wasn't really unusual. He was busy with his software start-up, and she rarely saw him these days.

The plan was to spend a few days over the Christmas break at his family home by the sea in Portland, and as long as he was at the hotel in the morning, that was fine.

She came from an outer-east Melbourne suburb nestled in the Dandenong Ranges, and found his beachside home and fishing family lifestyle utterly charming despite his complaints.

His dinner ticket, and the hotel room, were complimentary. He wouldn't know anyone at the Goldings Christmas Dinner, and she'd be working, so he probably wouldn't enjoy himself anyway.

But maybe they could get to know each other again while they were away. Rekindle their tired romance.

And if they couldn't, then maybe it was just time to move on.

After all, ten years after uni, they were very different people to the ones who'd met then.

But that was a problem for another day - she didn't have time to worry about the state of her relationship right at that moment.

Guests were starting to assemble as she slipped back into the room and made her way to the rear.

She could not help but notice the blonde man in the tailored dinner suit - he was literally head and shoulders above everyone else in the room.

Besides, his hair was curling around his collar, and it was so rare to see a curly headed man.

As her gaze lingered on his surfer sleek body, he must have felt it and turned around to look in her direction.

She quickly ducked and pretended to adjust her silver heeled Mary Janes. Amazingly comfortable *and* bought on sale.

But when she stood up again, he was still looking at her, with a gaze so dark and intense she had to hold a nearby chair for support.

And as she went through the remainder of the preparations for the dinner, she could feel him looking at her.

Every time she saw him from the corner of her eye, she couldn't help but turn to look, and she would see him looking back at her and once more avoid his gaze.

And every single time, she felt her heart flutter and her body flush.

It was clear she couldn't afford to get entangled with him. He was either the kind of man who didn't extend the first night to the second day, or the kind of man who demanded nothing short of surrender.

Either way, he was bad news, and threatened her hard won independence.

In her calculations, she completely forgot to factor in Max.

《《 • 》》

Ryan Griffith paused at the top of the stairs to look at the decorated room.

But not for long; he wasn't a Christmassy kind of guy.

The thing that did make him pause was the woman - he couldn't help but notice the woman.

For a start, she was wearing a very modest red dress. Longish sleeves, high neckline, and a long, wide skirt that clung to her legs without petticoats.

In a sea of tight, revealing, black dresses, you'd have to be blind not to notice her.

For a second, she'd bent over to do something to her shoe. A feat of some athleticism to bend from the waist, reaching the shoe without crouching.

She looked like a vintage ad for stockings, bent forward into an exceedingly pleasing R shape.

For a third, when she finally stood, cheeks slightly flushed, and shook her golden hair out, she looked like a fully clothed Botticelli's Venus. Would she be as lush as the painting underneath her dress?

He pulled himself together.

She looked like Christmas personified.

Then lost it again, thinking he was fully prepared to be her Santa any time she chose...

He shut his mouth with a snap.

Who, exactly, was she?

Not someone from Goldings, he was fairly sure he'd have noticed her; every beautiful woman in the place had approached him, and there were precious few whose outer beautify matched their inner.

Certainly no one he'd consider more than a couple of hours with, and he had a feeling his mystery woman was a keeper.

He descended the stairs, walked to the bar, and ordered a Whiskey Sour, swirling it absently in the glass as he watched her move around the room.

She didn't stop to speak with any of the assembled guests, just stood aside a little and waited for them to move on.

All the while scanning the crowd, perhaps looking for her date.

And then she stopped and spoke with a waiter, who indicated a hidden door through which she disappeared.

Not looking for her boyfriend then, but something to do with the event, perhaps managing it.

Someone from the hotel then.

Surely his mate Seth would've mentioned someone as gorgeous as that working here.

He sipped his drink, and waited for the woman to return. Chatting easily with his colleagues as they waited for drinks, but not encouraging anyone to linger.

The level in his drink glass gradually dropped, but she hadn't returned by the time the Master of Ceremonies had ascended the stage and invited the guests to be seated for the first course.

He strolled to the notice board, right of the bar, located his allocated table, and then found it.

Near the back, enticingly close to that hidden door.

But probably not close enough to be the recipient of any awards.

Not to worry, he hadn't planned to stay for the whole night anyway. Just to make an appearance, eat some of the extortionately priced dinner, and then leave.

He wouldn't have come at all, except he was obliged. These kind of events weren't really his thing.

As the table filled up, he traded inconsequentialities with his colleagues, until there were two seats left.

To his left.

With no name plates.

As the Master of Ceremonies started his patter, waiters circulated with glasses of champagne.

Welcome to the Goldings Annual Christmas Dinner. Evacuation exits here, here and here. Assembly areas there, there and there. Please welcome the band. The evening's agenda. The giving of Awards, and so on.

Ryan had heard it all so many times before he barely listened, just tilted his wrist to check the time and calculate how much longer before he could leave.

And then, in a cloud of sweet, floral perfume, the woman in the red dress sat next to him and laid a small red bag on the table.

Seeming not to notice the empty seat, she nodded politely to him, the man on her left, and the rest of table.

For a moment he was struck dumb, couldn't think of a single thing to say to her, and it filled him with dread.

Was he losing his touch?

Or possibly worse, was he that worried about making a hash of it?

The table stood to toast the successful year and the hope of the same for the new year.

He struggled to pull himself together and get his feet underneath him.

Telling himself to be cool.

As they sat again, she leaned slightly toward him, and thinking she wanted to talk, he leaned across to see what she had to say and their heads cracked together as they sat down.

Loud enough to make their dinner companions look to see the source of the sound.

She made a small sound of pain and put her hand up to touch her head, miscalculated the distance, and landed a blow to his jaw.

She made another small sound of pain.

He leaned away from her and rubbed his jaw, "that's quite a punch you have there!"

Her earnest brown eyes checked to see he was okay, "I'm so sorry, are you all right?"

"Yeah, I'm fine."

"Just as well," some wag across the table said, "wouldn't want to see you making an OHS claim this early in the evening."

Ryan glared across the table, unable to identify the speaker. Turning back to the woman, he asked, "what about you, are you okay?"

"Fine," she dropped her hand from her head, and turned the palm to face him, "see, no blood. It's all good.

"Wait," she said, her face shading towards white. She reached for her napkin, wrapping it around her hand, and holding it tight, "I think I caught your tooth on the way."

"I'll get some help," Ryan glanced around, looking for a waiter or someone else to call over for assistance, and when he turned back to her, she was half out of her chair.

"I'll just pop out the back and find the first aider. I know more or less where the kit should be."

As she cleared her chair, she stumbled as she caught the toe of her shoe in the hem of her skirt.

Ryan leapt up to help her, but she left him behind and almost sprinted across the small gap to disappear through the hidden door.

He looked around again, saw no one coming to help, but one or two guests looking curiously at him.

I'll just go make sure she's okay," he said, and scooping up her small bag, followed her through the door.

《《 • 》》

"Shit, shit, shit," Ava chanted as she trotted down the brightly lit service corridor towards the Conference Manager's office.

Not so much because she was injured, though she felt like her hand was on fire, but because she felt like she'd made a fool of herself.

A big fool.

The biggest fool.

She risked opening the napkin to look at her index finger and the back of her hand.

Still bleeding. She really hoped it didn't need stitches.

But it definitely needed a dressing of some kind.

Fortunately, the Night Event Manager, Seth, had given her a quick safety and security run down, so she knew he was the First Aider.

Luckily, he was in his office, so she didn't have to go looking for him or someone else to open the locked First Aid cabinet.

He rinsed the wound down with some saline, "looks nasty, what did you cut it on?"

"My chipped tooth," said someone behind her. She recognised the smell of his soap, and glanced over her shoulder to see the gorgeous man who'd cracked her head.

The Night Manager laughed, "I told you to go see a dentist Ryan," he said, then selected a couple of dressings from the kit.

He glanced up at her as he arranged the first one down her finger, "Ava have you met Ryan Griffith?"

She shook her head.

"Pleased to meet you," he said.

She smiled faintly and nodded her head, she had no plans to see him again.

Ever.

"Ava Gibson here's the Event Manager who organised Golding's Christmas Dinner," he told Ryan.

"You've done a good job."

Ava winced as Seth applied the second dressing around the edge of her hand.

"Sorry," Seth said. "this's partly my fault. I chipped his tooth at squash last week."

Ava attempted to smile through her gritted teeth, "you know each other then?" as if she cared about the answer.

"Best mates since high school," he wound a bandage around her hand and wrist to secure the dressing.

She grunted. It had hurt before, but after cleaning it, dressing it, and now compressing it, her hand was almost unbearably painful.

"There's quite a lot of blood, so you're probably going to need stitches. I've bound it fairly tightly, but I think you should go to the emergency room to get it looked at properly."

"I'll take you," said Ryan.

"Nonsense," she said, standing up, "I'm here to do a job, and I'm going to see it through."

A wave of dizziness hit her, and she sat down abruptly.

Ryan leapt across the room to steady her, and his hands burned like fire through the thin silk of her gown.

"Maybe I'll just go back to my room to lie down for a little while."

Seth put his palm across her forehead, "You're a bit warm, I really think you should go to hospital, but I can't force you."

"Perhaps tomorrow, if I still feel bad."

She stood, holding the back of the chair for support.

Seth shuffled some folders on his desk, picked one and quickly skimmed the contents. "Your notes are clear and concise, and now that food service's begun, there's nothing of great significance to be done, so don't be fretting about the rest of the party."

She nodded, winced and touched her head.

"Let me see you back to your room," Ryan said.

All Ava wanted to do was get to her room, but Seth clapped Ryan's shoulder, "good man, make sure she's okay."

And to Ava, "do you want me to get some soup or something sent to your room?"

"No thanks. I just want to go lie down. Thanks Seth."

Seth nodded, "try to keep the bandage elevated."

Ryan slipped an arm around her shoulders. Standing next to him, she realised he was even more ridiculously tall than she'd thought.

Romances would call her petite, or some such nonsense, but compared to him, she was a dwarf.

Bashful most likely.

And not entirely sure that his proximity wasn't the entire reason she felt dizzy rather than a knock on the head in conjunction with the hand trauma.

Compared to Max, he was tall *and* strong.

She was the strong one in their relationship - any jars that needed opening, she opened them. Spiders that needed removing from the bath, also her. Not to mention putting the bins out.

Or just bloody going out and earning a living.

Just for a moment, she allowed herself to snuggle into the warmth under his shoulder.

To lean on him, letting herself imagine he would take care of her.

To place her wounded hand alongside his heart, imagining she could feel it beat, slowly and steadily beneath her fingers.

All too soon, they arrived at her room.

"Key?" he asked.

She fished it out of her bag and gave it to him, smothering a small smile at the notional chivalry of the gesture.

He insert it in the digital lock, she heard it click.

He paused, lowered door handle in his hand.

He was taking too long, so she leaned around him and pushed the door with her left hand.

She took him by surprise, and he fell in through the door.

He hooked an arm around her waist and swung her against his chest as he turned his back to the room.

"What the hell do you think you're doing?" she demanded.

And only then did she hear the voice of a woman, "Max, don't stop, I'm nearly there."

She tried to look around Ryan's body, but he held her firm. She looked up at him and he shook his head.

Ava forced his arms open and his body out of her way, and watched her boyfriend try to disentangle himself from some red-headed woman.

She heard ringing in her ears and felt a sharp pain in her head. She struggled to put her hand to her head, took a step, and watched the floor rise up to meet her.

Ryan panicked as she fell over, but managed to grab a hold of her before she hit the floor.

He watched the man try to disentangle himself from the woman for a moment, then opened the door and supported Ava through it.

Letting the door close, he shrugged her into a more comfortable position, cradling her in his arms.

He strode back down the corridor, fighting off a red haze of fury.

With whichever one of those people was Ava's partner. Hell, both of them!

With Seth for not ensuring she went to hospital.

And with himself for not stopping her from seeing what was going on in the room.

He pushed the button for a lift, and thankfully, the carriage was waiting where they'd left it.

As the doors slid closed, the man from Ava's room, still trying to get his pants on was trying to run down the corridor.

"Wait! Who are you? What are you doing with my girlfriend."

Max then.

Bloody check of him calling Ava his girlfriend given what he'd just been doing.

With *another* woman.

Coming out on the ground floor, he went straight for the taxi rank rather than calling a valet to get his car.

He didn't want her so called boyfriend finding her before she'd had a chance to think in peace.

And to get the appropriate treatment.

That slimy bastard boyfriend probably had some kind of pathetic excuse.

"Royal Melbourne Hospital," he said as he stowed her safely in the back seat and climbed in beside her. He fastened her seatbelt as the cab pulled away.

"What happened?" the driver asked.

"Cut her hand and hit her head. Concussion I think."

The driver indicated, "should've called an ambulance mate," he said as he paused waiting for the traffic to clear.

"No time. Probably quicker this way anyway."

The driver nodded, and sped up the car a little, weaving in and around the traffic.

Before too long, the were pulling up outside the hospital.

Ryan threw a bunch of twenties at the driver, "keep the change," he said as he released the seatbelt and slid her out.

"She's lucky to have a guy like you," the driver said, toasting him with the cash, "good luck mate."

Ryan nodded, and carried her into the emergency department.

Unfortunately, being Friday night, the place was packed.

The noise of drunk or drugged young men screaming was deafening, and the chaos was almost enough to make him back away and take her somewhere else.

There were no seats available, even if he'd been prepared to leave her unattended.

Ava weighed barely more than a mouse, so for the moment at least, he was content to hold her in his arms.

Happily, a nurse approached him, and after hearing what had happened, brought him through to a large, cool, air-conditioned ward and invited him to lay Ava on a bed.

"We'll need to get her gown off," he said, "are you comfortable taking care of that?"

Ryan blushed, and stuttered something, and the nurse laughed.

"I'll get one of my female colleagues to take care of it."

A short while later a female nurse ushered him out, and a short while after that, he was invited back into the cubicle.

Ava was tucked into a hospital gown and the blanket drawn up to her waist.

Her dress was neatly folded on the chair along with her shoes and stockings.

The nurse checked her temperature, blood pressure and pulse, flashed a torch in her eyes, and started filling out the admission forms.

Not that Ryan was able to help with much of them - name, but no medical history, Medicare details or contact details.

"I'm happy to go guarantor until you can speak with her," he said.

She nodded, "Doctor will be with you shortly," she said as she drew the curtains around the sides of the bed.

Ryan looked around at the grubby ward, the bustling staff, and didn't know what to do with himself.

He took his tie off and tucked it into his jacket pocket, then packed her dress and shoes inside his jacket like a gift, and held it in his lap as he dropped into the chair next to her bed.

"Hang in there kiddo," he said, taking her hand.

It seemed like forever before a doctor came to see them, pushing a mobile steel cabinet with drawers before her.

She checked Ava's chart as she introduced herself, "I'm Doctor Stephenson, can you tell me what happened?"

Ryan quickly related the events of the evening, as the young woman rinsed her hands in an alcohol solution and slipped on some gloves.

She unwrapped the bandage from Ava's right hand, and dropped it in a medical waste bag hanging off the back of the cabinet.

Putting on her safety glasses she examined the wound, "your First Aider's done a good job, but it definitely needs stitches."

She put a disposable towel on a tray on top of the cabinet, pulled a bunch of dressings together on the tray along with a threaded needle.

She injected a local anaesthetic, and dropped the syringe in the sharps bin at the other end of the cabinet.

Then cleaned the cut again, and put in five stitches.

As she moved onto dressing and bandaging the wound, Ryan said, "Look, I don't actually know her, but she's just finished managing a major event so I'd wager she's not been eating or sleeping as well as she could've been."

The doctor glanced at him, frowned, and then nodded.

She added a cannula to the tray then inserted it into the back of Ava's left hand. "I'll order some blood tests to check her levels, and I'll administer some antibiotics via a drip."

She finished dressing the wound, winding the bandage around the hand and partway up her arm, when he was done she placed it on Ava's chest.

"Try to keep her hand elevated above the heart as long as you can, and you can take the bandage off tomorrow."

Ryan nodded.

She folded the towel like an envelope over the packaging left on the tray and dropped it in the bin. Then wrote a bunch of stuff on the chart.

"It's all good," she said stripping off her gloves and tossing them in the bin. "We'll keep her here for an hour or two, and then decide whether to transfer her to a ward or release her. The nurse will be back in a moment with the drip."

She left the cubicle, and moved onto the next.

For the moment at least, he and Ava were more or less alone.

Aside from the beeping machines, the moans of other patients, and the quite hum of conversation.

He closed his eyes, rested his head on Ava's legs, and listened to the late night sound of the emergency department.

He found himself silently chanting, "please be okay. Please be okay. Please be okay."

A nurse woke him by bustling into the cubicle. He quickly connected up the drip, then injected the antibiotics into it.

"No response yet?"

"Not yet."

He applied a tourniquet, drew blood, and released the constriction.

"I shouldn't worry, it's still fairly early."

Ryan nodded.

Surprised by the strength of his desire to protect her.

Not just from the fallout of her traumatic injury, but from her boyfriend's infidelity as well.

Once more he laid his forehead on her legs, and willed her to wake up and get better.

《《 • 》》

When Ava woke, she was surprised to be in a hospital ward with off-white by grey walls and floor.

Even more surprised to be dressed in a hospital gown.

She panicked, plucked at the bed covers to pull them higher, and noticed the cannula in her hand.

Then she saw her dress, on a hanger, hanging on the inside of the curtain rail where she could see it, and relaxed.

Ahead of her there was a gap in the curtains through which she could see red and purple streaked skies though a large window, and assumed it was dawn the next day.

Quiet conversation came from outside the room, and the sound of soft snoring from within.

Her hand was warm and snug in a man's grasp, "Max," she croaked quietly.

And then she realised the hair was blonde and curly, not straight and mouse-brown.

His white shirt was open at the neck, and he'd rolled up his sleeves.

She glanced around to see his jacket was slung over the back of the hospital chair, and he'd tucked his bow tie in the pocket.

From her vantage point it looked to be a tie-it-yourself bow tie rather than the ready-made kind.

She smiled, remembering how she used to tie them for her father, and being disappointed that Max found them too complicated and preferred ready-made.

Even though they never sat quite right on him.

Then again, she'd already checked out the tailoring of his potentially bespoke suit.

A little larger in the shoulders, arms and legs to accommodate his muscles. And a little trimmer in the waist and hips to form a pleasingly triangular silhouette.

As her brain ticked through the differences, she realised he was Ryan Griffith - the man she'd been attracted too from the Golding's dinner.

She felt a little curl of heat within her as she contemplated her relative lack of clothing protection.

Ava wanted to pull her hand away, but at the same time, she wanted to hold it tightly and never let it go.

Max had been all the future she'd imagined.

He was her first major crush, and she'd been so overcome by love for him, she'd lost all interest in any kind of career or education.

Romanticising caring for his home and kids, she'd withdrawn from Uni to take care of him.

Never once broadened her thinking to wonder whether she, herself, was happy with that.

And recalling what she'd seen the night before, he'd probably never thought seriously about her future either.

It was the harshest of possible lessons, and she wondered if she could get past that.

Wondered if she could forgive him.

Pick up where she'd left off, visit his parents for Christmas, stay with him and forget that she'd caught him *in flagrante.*

Mind you, if she'd caught him once, how often had he been with other women while they were supposed to be together?

And was it something he would keep doing?

Most likely.

Just not in her work-related hotel room.

She grimaced – he had such poor judgement.

So much wiser to go somewhere else and not risk getting caught.

Did he think she was so stupid she wouldn't notice the rumpled sheets or the smell of another woman's perfume?

Though maybe she already had, countless times after a long hard day at work.

Was it time to think about moving on without Max in her life?

She turned her focus towards Ryan Griffith.

She'd met him less than twenty-four hours ago, and he was currently asleep on her leg, clutching her hand in his.

Perhaps he wasn't the playboy she had assumed.

Gippsland dairy farm boy made good?

From running around after cows to running around share trading and floating companies at Goldings?

Or did he have an overdeveloped sense of duty.

Despite her experience with Max, she couldn't stop herself from imagining a golden future with Ryan Griffith.

Early morning trips to Sorrento beach to go surfing. Cruising the lanes for cocktails. Antiquing in Tyabb.

His naked body entwined with hers.

And later, lithe beautiful children, blonde haired and sun bronzed who looked just like him.

Adorable.

Now that she was fully awake, she needed a drink of water.

And the bathroom.

Not necessarily in that order.

She looked around and over her shoulders to find out where the drip was, and of course it was attached to the bed.

Turning around to look at Ryan to gauge the possibility of moving him, she noticed one eye was open, and it was looking at her.

She blushed.

He smiled a lazy, half-asleep smile, "mornin."

"I need some help with the bathroom."

And then it was his turn to blush, and she laughed.

"Not using it, just getting the drip down so I can go."

"Not that I wouldn't if you needed me to," he said, getting up to pull it down, " but I'm relieved you don't."

He held the bag for her, and held out a hand to steady her as she approached the edge of the bed and eased off it onto the floor.

Then he walked with her to the bathroom tucked into the corner of the room, and waited outside while she used it.

When she was done, she washed her hands and couldn't help noticing she looked a fright.

Even without the drip bag between her teeth.

"You look like the Wreck of the Hesperus," she told herself as she tried to finger-comb her hair into some kind of order.

Then gave it up as a bad job and settled for rinsing her mouth and splashing her face with water.

She glanced doubtfully in the mirror again, and wasn't entirely sure she'd improved the situation.

Still, he'd seen her worse.

One last go at her hair, and she reminded herself he'd seen her better too.

《《 • 》》

Ryan had watched her sleep, on and off throughout the night.

Trying to think of a way to keep her with him longer.

Could he invite her for breakfast? Maybe she'd find the hospital breakfast to her liking.

And even if she didn't, where could he take her? Was inviting her to his apartment too forward?

He knocked on the bathroom door, "are you okay in there."

A muffled reply came from within, which he took as reassurance she was okay.

A short time later, she came out, and he took the drip back from her, fixing it back to the bed as she hopped into it.

"What's the time?"

He checked his watch, "six am."

"You know, I didn't get anything to eat last night, and I'm absolutely starving."

"I can go down to the ground floor café and get you something if you like."

"Do you think they'd have a bacon sandwich?"

He shrugged.

"Maybe a toasted ham, cheese and tomato sandwich then; I can pay you back okay?"

"I think I can spring you a toasted sandwich seeing as I almost killed you."

She snorted, "you did not."

"I dunno, it was touch and go for a while there."

She sobered instantly, "was it?"

He nudged her shoulder, "hey, I'm kidding!"

She put her uninjured hand on her chest, "you had me going for a while there."

"Clearly you need some food - would you prefer tea or coffee?"

"Latte please, no sugar."

"Then I shall fetch your order forthwith," he bowed ostentatiously.

Grabbing his wallet from his jacket, he saluted her and left the room.

Filled with a sudden burst of energy, he took the stairs, jumping down two at a time.

And as he reached the café, he caught the smell of frying bacon, and smiled. He ordered the toasted sandwich, a bacon sandwich, and two of the biggest size lattes.

The café was packed with people in scrubs, so his order took a little while, and he fretted about Ava as he paced up and down the length of the counter.

And when it was done, and packed into a carry bag, he stuffed a bunch of sauce sachets in too, and walked back up the stairs.

She was sitting up when he got back.

Someone had moved the table across the bed, and gotten her a water jug, a cup of something he supposed might have been coffee, and a couple of packets of biscuits.

"I have hunted," he said as he walked through the door, "and I have returned victorious."

She laughed, and the sound was so bright and cheerful and alive, he wanted to hear more of it.

"So," he said as he unpacked, "I got both sandwiches, so you can take your pick."

She made a grab for the latte and took a long drink of coffee, before she answered, smacking her lips and saying, "aahhh, I needed that.

"You must be hungry too, why don't we both have half of each?"

"Oh. I hadn't thought about it, but I just realised I am."

It might have seemed obvious to her, but Ryan thought it was kind.

He wracked his brain trying to think of the last time someone had been spontaneously kind to him.

And that was actually impossible; investment banking wasn't the kind of field that generally attracted kind people.

She picked up one wrapped packet and handed the other to him, tearing open the layers of papers to reveal the sandwich. "Bacon," she said, "is there any brown sauce?"

He shuffled through the sauce packets, "tomato... or... barbecue."

He watched, faintly horrified and disgusted as she reached for the barbecue, lifted the top slice of bread and squirted it over the bacon.

"It's really nice! Really. Do you want to try it?" she held the sandwich out to him.

He made a face, but leaned over and took a bite, chewing slowly and cautiously, but she was right.

It was tasty.

He grunted and nodded his head, "not sure I'll be giving up tomato sauce just yet."

He sipped some coffee, then unwrapped the toasted ham, cheese and tomato. Moaning a little as he enjoyed the first bite.

They enjoyed their coffee and the rest of the sandwiches in a companionable silence.

Ava was kind of relaxing to be around.

No demands for attention or feats of indulgence.

Nor did she insist of filling the air with the sound of her voice, for the sake of hearing it.

He wondered whether her boyfriend was the drama queen in that relationship, and once more felt a wave of anger that he was taking the gorgeous woman sitting in front of him for granted.

"Any idea when I can get out of here?" she asked.

"What? No.

"Sorry, when they moved you to the ward, the doctor said they'll assess you this morning, and then decide."

"Ah," she wiped her hands on a napkin. "And why did they decide to admit me?"

"You were dehydrated, and something about levels, and something about the stitches."

She raised one eyebrow, and he loved her for it.

He shrugged, "I didn't understand three-quarters of it. I'm just glad they didn't accuse me of giving you tetanus!"

She laughed again.

Not long after they'd finished eating, the doctor and a gaggle of students came to check Ava, and he was banished until they'd completed the check.

As the doctor left, he told Ryan, "the bandage can come off this morning, and we'll put some dressings on, but don't let them get wet. For pain relief, a couple of paracetamol tablets four hourly, or as needed."

He nodded and the flock moved on.

Ava rolled her eyes at him as he entered the room.

"Typical telling the guy what needs to be done. Now we just have to wait for the nurse to take care of the bandages and we can go," she said.

《《 • 》》

Almost as soon as the words were out of her mouth, Ava winced.

Much as she liked the idea of him sticking around, she had no right to assume he would.

He wasn't her boyfriend.

And then she remembered what she'd seen the night before again. And where exactly was the cheater?

"Where's Max?" she asked.

His face reddened as he sat on the edge of the chair.

He averted his eyes, and picked at a fingernail. "He aah, well I...

"Look I'm sorry to be crude, and maybe overstepping your boundaries, but he was shagging some girl, and I didn't want him here with you begging for forgiveness, or telling you it was a mistake, or he never meant to hurt you, or whatever. I didn't want him stressing you out and distracting you from getting the care you needed."

It *was* kind of high-handed, but Max would have done exactly what Ryan thought he might.

By the time she left hospital, he would probably have talked her around, and she would have gone with him out of habit.

And when, for that matter, had Max last shagged *her*?

She sighed.

"So I saw what I thought I saw."

"Yes."

"And did you..." she waved up at the dress.

His colour had been returning to normal, but he blushed again, "oh no. Oh god no. One of the nurses took care of that."

She laughed at his embarrassment, and couldn't resist teasing him, "so you wouldn't want too..."

He sucked in his breath, and looked at her, "I didn't say that. I just said that at this time, in this particular location, I didn't undress you."

It was the oddest thing, she'd thought his eyes were bright blue, but as she looked into their depths, she realised they were a more of a deep teal colour.

He leaned towards her, looked searchingly into her eyes, "trust me, when the right time comes, I won't hesitate to take your clothes off one by one."

She wasn't really aware that she'd leaned closer towards him.

But thankfully, or maybe not, a nurse chose that moment to walk in, "I'm here to take out the... Oh, do you guys want me to come back later."

Ryan leaned back with, was that disappointment on his face?

Ava knew she was disappointed, though what she'd hoped might happen was another thing.

Quite possibly best not pursued in a shared hospital ward.

She sat back, "no. I'm more than ready to get out of here."

"I bet you are," the nurse said with a wink, "I'll try to be as quick as I can. I'll take care of the drip first, then check the wound."

And to Ryan, "if you'd excuse us please?" She waited until he'd left the room.

Ava looked at the door, and wished he'd stayed behind.

What the hell was it going to be like to let him go.

The nurse clamped off the drip, removed it from the cannula, and pulled the tape loose.

She picked up a cotton wool ball, held it in place, then pulled the attachment out. "Put some pressure on this will you?" she asked as she disposed of the drip and cannula.

Then she checked it, "all good," and put a tiny padded sticker on the insertion point.

"Now let's check the stitches." She unwound the bandage, found there was no blood, either on it or the dressings beneath.

"I just need to make sure there's no signs of infection in the wound," she said, gently removing the dressings and nodding. "Nice and neat," she said approvingly, taping it up with another dressing.

She told Ava how to care for it, and as she left the room, she heard her telling Ryan how to take care of it too.

She smiled ruefully at him as he re-entered the room, and he winked at her.

"Another pair of ears is always good," he said, "so you can leave now?"

She swallowed the sudden lump in her throat.

Clearly she'd got the wrong idea, and he wanted to be rid of her.

Now she had to think of what to do with her day - she couldn't go home, and she couldn't go back to the hotel.

And without doing either of those things, she had nothing aside from her dinner gown and high heels to wear.

She couldn't go anywhere without people looking at her, and assuming she'd been out all night with some guy.

And while she had, it wasn't the kind of out with a guy that anyone would be imagining.

She couldn't buy anything, because she didn't have any cash or a credit card, as she'd planned on staying in the function hotel.

God it was a nightmare, but better to get the pain over before it got any worse.

"Yes. Don't feel obliged to stay, I can manage."

Damn it, her lip quivered and her eyes filled with tears. She swallowed again, and closed her eyes.

And felt a tear ease out of her closed lids and turned away.

He sat on the edge of the bed, and smoothed the tear away with the pad of his thumb.

"I don't want to leave you like this," he said.

"So. Um... Um... I...

"Would you like to go out for lunch with me?"

She smiled, because as it turned out, he did want to spend time with her.

And also because it didn't seem to matter to him whether or not he looked or sounded like an idiot with her.

At least not at that moment.

She so wanted to kiss him right then.

Instead, she said, "why don't you step outside and I'll get dressed."

He grinned, "I'm looking forward to seeing you again," and stepped out.

Ava did a little dance, then pulled off the hospital gown, pulled her dress off its hanger, and hurriedly got dressed.

She didn't want to waste any time. Or risk him leaving without her.

Ryan ducked out of the room, and did a little happy dance of his own.

He couldn't believe he'd almost let her blow him off like that.

If he hadn't seen that tear, he would've left, assuming she didn't want to see him.

It didn't bear thinking about.

He put his hand over his heart and tried to imagine how awful that Ava shaped hole would be.

They'd barely spoken to each other, yet... he couldn't imagine a life without her in it.

The comfortable silences, the feel of her perfect fit under his arm, and her seemingly ravenous appetite for bacon.

The unaffected glimpses of her bare shoulder as the gown slipped off it, and the curve of her back seen through the gap in the back of it.

He laughed, and turned around, just in time to see her walk out the room.

If it was at all possible, she looked more beautiful in the daylight.

He gasped. Even after being admitted to hospital for a night, she took his breath away, and he did not want to let her out of his sight again.

"Just let me get my things," he said, ducking back into the room for his jacket, throwing it on and patting the pocket to make sure the wallet was there.

"Anything else?" he asked, and she shook her head shyly.

He held out his hand, and after a pause, she took it and he felt the hairs on his arm stand on end.

Her hand fit perfectly in the palm of his.

The lift was crowded, but he pulled her in close to the edge and shielded her with his body.

And soon, they were standing hand in hand, just outside the Grattan Street forecourt.

He wanted to run down the street, holding her hand, and jump into a tram as if he was in a 1950s movie, but the streams of cars and pedestrians and traffic lights forbade it.

Not to worry. She was there with him, and at least he could savour the closeness.

"So what's next?" he asked.

She swung his arm back and forth as she thought about it. "I can't go to the hotel, and I can't go home, but I've discovered I'm exhausted."

She yawned widely, and he smothered a yawn himself.

"I don't want to seem overly pushy, but if I can't take you to yours, do you want to come to mine?"

"I thought you'd never ask," she said so impishly, he laughed.

"Very well then," let's go outside and see if we can get a taxi.

She shivered in the cool morning air, so he took his jacket off and slid it around her shoulders where it was almost knees length on her. Adorably so.

Impulsively he dropped a kiss on the top of her head.

They didn't manage to get the first taxi they saw, but after a couple of attempts they were on the way.

He slipped an arm around her shoulder as they moved though the City and out the other side, stopping at his Queens Road apartment building.

He paid the driver, and gave Ava a moment to look out over Albert Park.

"I run around the lake every morning," he said.

She turned to look at him critically, "it shows."

She looked back, "your apartment must have cost a tonne of money."

"Not as much as it's worth now," he said with an ironic smile, and moved his arm to gesture towards to building.

Seemingly overawed, she clutched his hand as she moved towards the building.

The lift was swift and silent, and as usual he was grateful for that.

Perhaps even more so with Ava on board.

He opened the door, and stepped back to let her go first, grinning a little as she absorbed the panoramic view of Albert Park and Port Phillip Bay.

She walked across the Living/Dining room, opened the sliding door and walked out onto the balcony.

"How do you get anything done around here with that view?"

He lightly rested his hands on her shoulders, "it is distracting," he said, meaning her.

She snorted, seeming to understand.

"Do you want to take a shower? I can find you a t-shirt of mine to wear."

"Actually yes," she said.

Back in the apartment he found her a clean t-shirt to wear, a clean towel and unopened tablet of soap to use. He took them out to her, "care to see the facilities?"

While she showered in the guest bathroom, he showered in the ensuite.

When he emerged in track pants and a t-shirt, she was already curled up, asleep in his bed.

He folded the bedspread over the top of her, and debated about staying there, or moving to the guest room.

But stripped of make-up, she seemed younger. More innocent.

He lay next to her, closed his eyes, and drifted off.

He woke to find himself half under the covers, with Ava a warm solid presence behind him.

Her arm was wound around him, and she was stroking his leg with her foot.

It was kind of nice.

He wriggled around as he rolled over so he could see her face, trying not to hurt her injured hand.

They looked at each other for a long moment, before he leaned towards her, testing.

When she didn't draw away, he leaned a little closed and brushed her lips with his.

He widened the gap again and searched her face.

No shock or revulsion, but there was something softer about her. He couldn't say for sure what it was, but he kissed her again.

For a little longer.

She broke the kiss, and looked at him steadily, "you could have anyone."

He shrugged one shoulder, "I don't want anyone, I want you."

She laughed.

"Honestly, I can't believe I didn't know you existed yesterday. I feel like I've known you forever."

"Then shut up and kiss me."

«« • »»

Some time later, Ava's stomach rumbled.

"Are you hungry again already?"

She patted her stomach and grinned, "I sure am! I've been so busy in the last few days, I've hardly had time to eat! And once I've eaten, I've decisions to make."

Ryan leaned on one elbow, "you should stay here," he blurted out.

"Can I?"

He nodded.

"That would make this the best Christmas ever!"

One decision down, she flung herself on him again, and they didn't surfaced for some time.

THE END

CHRISTMAS CONFLAGRATION

Matilda May McDonald was the crazy cat lady.

The fact that she didn't have any cats didn't seem to matter to the rest of the village.

Nor the fact that she owned four dogs; an Alsatian called Nellie, a Spaniel named Blackie, a Kelpie called Cobber, and a Yorkie named Billie.

Generally, when Matilda saw cats hanging around her place, she let the dogs loose to chase them off.

And when she saw them on the street, she hissed and told them to SCRAM.

But, as far as the village was concerned, the only fact that mattered was that Matilda lived in a ramshackle, half falling down house, with an overgrown garden.

And that she appeared at least 105!

Matilda, known as Tilly to her friends, was actually only 55, but had fully enjoyed her sun-drenched, tiny bikini-clad youth at the beach.

The one she had to take a bus and two trains to get to.

The consequent sun damage was so severe she required biannual dermatology appointments to have the resulting cancers frozen off, which gave her skin an unfortunate scarred and pockmarked appearance due to the blistering.

Though this was much better than the crescent-shaped surgical scar on her face, the trigger for the dermatology appointments in the first place.

And the reason why she didn't care for any further surgeries.

In the main, Tilly preferred "crazy cat lady" to the historical alternative of "witch."

The village was more tolerant of crazy cat ladies than witches, and there were fewer incidents of ringing the doorbell and running away, faecal infernos on the door-mat, and less stone-throwing.

She'd lived alone most of her life; her husband-to-be having got frozen feet and left her at the altar with no explanation or further contact, after which point, she swore off men altogether.

Only rarely did a semi-educated person call her Miss Havisham, and then only once, as Matilda had grown a ruthless streak that didn't allow second chances.

Having lived alone for such a long time, she had developed the habit of talking to herself.

And holding one-sided conversations with the cockatoos, magpies, and possums she shared her garden with.

And the occasional wandering echidna.

Not forgetting the night-time conversations with owls, Australian fruit bats, and foxes.

Who were coincidentally, three-quarters of the way responsible for how overgrown the garden was.

And even Tilly was aware of the irony given people like her are sometimes referred to as fruit bats.

Talking to herself *had* been a problem.

But after watching a couple of episodes of *Continuum*, she started wearing a Bluetooth headset when she was out which at least meant people weren't staring at her.

Well, given the way she generally dressed, not much anyway.

She had a... let's say... distinctive way of dressing.

In her younger days, the late nineties and early oughties, she'd bought a lot of clothes.

Most of them fairly well made, so she'd never seen a need to update her image with more recently fashionable clothes she didn't much like.

Perhaps in America or England someone would've sent her on a makeover show, but not here in Australia.

Tilly particularly loved leopard print, unstructured granny dresses, flannies, boot cut jeans, leggings, and low-cut matching tracksuits.

And to match them; platform heels, Doc Martens and cowboy boots.

For that matter, having mismatched nail art when it wasn't fashionable, or ironic, probably wasn't helping matters either.

Anyone seeing her, and not the professional nail job, would quite rightly think she was either homeless or living in a squat somewhere.

Though to be perfectly honest, she'd inherited the squat house when her parents had ended their lives driving off a long, straight stretch of rural highway into the only tree for miles around while she was away at university.

Her profession was social work, and she worked in the community.

Her shambolic appearance, which to be honest she didn't see anything wrong with, was an excellent way of disarming what many "normal" people would also consider the "crazies."

She was in the habit of bringing said "crazies" into her home; human and animal both.

The four previously mentioned dogs and currently five mismatched, misplaced and misunderstood humans.

The villagers would have been scandalised if they knew, but like any "normal" person, they tended to avert their gaze and not look directly at what was going on at the crazy cat lady's house.

Some of them made gestures to ward off bad luck as they walked by.

Fat lot of good it did them too.

Tilly's property was situated on a large plot of about ten acres of mostly wild eucalypt and fern forest on the outskirts of town, so there wasn't a great deal of casual walking past anyway.

She and her five... house guests had been preparing for Christmas.

Not that any of them were particularly Christmas oriented people who liked a good party with friends and family.

Being more of the kind of people who need quiet time alone as much, if not more than shelter, food and water.

However, they were aware that being seen to not be fully on board with Christmas was a sure-fire way to quench the milk of human kindness of approximately 99.5% of "normal" people.

So they hung decorations, and because Tilly was the only one with a job, prepared handmade gifts crafted from the largess of the land.

Sadly, it takes a special kind of person to appreciate a handmade gift these days. And we're not talking about macaroni necklaces or sad scribbles masquerading as art.

We're talking about actual art; sticks whittled into charming representations of animals, charcoal landscape drawings, and scarves knitted from possum and other furs (including dog and cat) caught in the fencing wires around Tilly's property.

And my personal favourite, a lovingly handcrafted story written by a child of my acquaintance, (I expect it'll be worth something one day).

Is it odd, I wonder, that the most creative people are also the craziest?

Even sadder to my mind, the "crazies" were making a lot of art to sell at the village craft market in the hope of making enough money to purchase something wonderful that Tilly would love.

And to look at it, and know wihout doubt she was loved by others.

Which is ironic, because she *was* that special kind of person who loves handmade art.

Especially the kind that comes from the heart and not through an agent who makes all the money in the exchange.

And perhaps it was that they were all working on their own projects, and not the *really* bad TV reception that meant they were unaware the famous Evangelist Brother Jimmy Marrs would be visiting the village for one night only the week before Christmas.

Had they known, they might have gone because they thought he'd be good for a laugh.

They might even have bathed before arriving.

And had that been the case, they would almost certainly have been doomed.

But as it was, Tilly and her four dogs and five crazy humans slept blissfully through the night. Waking up the next day in a universe that was similar in many ways to their own, but quite different in several key respects.

The main one being that Tilly had lost her crazy cat lady status, and become something far worse than a witch.

She had become the source of all the villages woes; a scapegoat.

Not that any of the villagers would have been able to adequately explain what exactly their woes were.

Only the Jimmy Marrs of this world can do that.

They settled for grumbling about her and the effect she had on the village, (which the day before had been nothing).

Grumbling turned to complaining.

And complaining to carping.

Via envy, through jealousy and onto vicious fault-finding.

Malcontented escalated further to offended and onwards to disaffected.

Like the most virulent of viruses spreading through the community, until nothing would satisfy them but blood.

Within twenty-four hours they had worked themselves into a frenzy.

Coming together at the local church for Carols by Candlelight.

Mrs Van Beek had decorated the church for the annual event with red and green arrangements of Australian natives gathered from local gardens and bushland.

Including southern cypress, woolly bushes, and gum leaves, interspersed with red bottlebrushes, holly-leaved grevilleas and Christmas Bells.

And of course, candles.

The old-fashioned kind you had to light on fire.

Despite there being a Total Fire Ban.

Despite it being a Code Red fire danger day.

She thought they'd be safe because she used tulip shaped wind protectors that also capture the hot wax droplets.

It was sweltering that night, so they opened all the doors and windows to let what passed for a breeze into the church.

The breeze that was not even enough to set the candles flickering.

It was a lovely, though not exactly tuneful night.

The high school band played, and the local primary school choir sang.

Local girl made good, opera singer Maggie Moore, sang a couple of songs, encouraging the audience to sing along.

And when it was over, they found the fridge had packed up, but they took their lukewarm beer and wine, with the cheese sweating in the heat into the church garden and ate and drank it anyway.

And of course, that was somehow Tilly's fault as well.

They looked up the hill, and plain as day, there was Tilly's house looking back at them.

All the windows blazing with light, as though she was defiantly not attending church.

Boldly refusing to contribute to the community by buying drinks and raffle tickets.

Challenging the community to do something about it.

One by one, they stood and assembled in a huddle on the lawn looking up.

They were sweltering in the heat.

Befuddled by drink.

Ill with the bad cheese, though they didn't know it yet.

Filled with savage and bitter resentment.

Someone has to do something they agreed.

And then someone did.

Scorned suitor Baz Bell stalked into the church, grabbed a candle and started striding up the hill.

And one by one, the others did the same, until there were no more candles.

Running to fall in behind Baz.

And those without candles were carried away in the rush.

It is a testament to the power of their false bravado that they walked for fifteen minutes uphill until they reached Tilly's place.

They attributed the darkness of the windows to Tilly hiding like the coward they thought she was.

Baz broke stride at the fence, yet forged onward up the long drive. Stopping half or dozen or so paces from the house.

The villagers caught up.

Face working, Baz hurled the candle, protector and all, at the house.

The villagers followed suit shortly after; a barrage of flaming candles.

It had been a fairly dry year, and the house was clad in dusty, leaf and twig decorated spider webs.

They went up like a tinderbox, dropping fiery leaves into the dead garden beds beneath.

Candle flame licked the garden before deciding it liked the taste and consuming it all.

The leaf litter on the ground caught light, smouldering until finally, a hot breeze rose up.

Embers blew around the villagers, setting fire to the twigs, leaves and the shedding bark of the trees.

The villagers were able to swot and stamp out the embers that threatened them, but they couldn't fo anything about those that settled into the leaf stuffed gutters.

Tiny fires set in the small branches, and grew to the larger branches, and before they knew what was happening, the forest exploded in a whirlwind of insects, birds, and small mammals fleeing in all directions.

After a short, stunned pause, Tilly startled them by smashing open the French Doors on the front sitting room.

Four dogs and five humans erupted out of the blazing house.

The villagers abruptly sobered up.

Waking up from the pernicious teachings of Brother Jimmy Marrs.

And less than four and a half minutes after Baz had thrown the first candle, it was already too late.

The flames had engulfed the house, and with the stiffening breeze coming up the hill, pushing the fire ahead of itself, the blaze caught up with the volatile gases from the gum trees; they could see fireballs exploding just above the fire as it raced uphill.

Baz Bell dropped to his knees and howled as he realised what he had done.

You see, Baz was the captain of the local Fire Brigade, and this incident would see him imprisoned for arson.

Worse, for him, barred from the fire fighting forces forever.

Tilly on the other hand laughed.

She laughed until she cried.

She laughed until she couldn't stand up any longer and fell to her knees as well.

She laughed until she couldn't breathe and her breath came in sobbing gasps.

The villagers hustled around her, thinking the poor crazy cat lady was in shock.

They picked her up and carried her away down the driveway.

What the villagers didn't know, was that Tilly laughed because she was free.

Free of the parents who'd cursed her to live a life she hated.

Free of the chains that bound her to her past.

Free to travel, to meet new people, to do whatever she wanted.

That was why she'd never spent any money on the house or land.

She'd wanted it condemned so she could knock it down, even though she wasn't sure that would be enough to end the curse.

But with the house and land razed by the fierceness of the fire, it was enough.

Someone called emergency services, and the wail of sirens and prayers was soon answered by heavy rain.

First, the rain evaporated as it met the flames, and then it steamed as it met the ground, and just as the fire brigade finally arrived with ambulances in tow, it was setting in puddles on the ground.

And when the authorities asked how it started, Tilly said she didn't know.

That the villagers had run up the hill to help.

And the villagers were thankful and found places for herself, her dogs and her humans.

They took up a collection and sent her to a day spa, a hairdresser, and bought her some new fashionable clothes.

And when she came back, they barely recognised her.

It was Baz Bell who asked, "Tilly, is that you?"

And so the villagers forgot the crazy cat lady and she became Tilly once more.

When the insurance money came through, she put it in the bank.

And when the property sold, to a developer of retirement villages, she put the money in the bank.

And when the time came, she packed a small bag and bought a one-way plane ticket out of there.

Though Baz still receives postcards from strange and exotic locations, and he hopes that one day soon, she might come home.

THE END

I had the most disturbing dream.

Or maybe it was a memory...

I was in a scuffed meeting room with pale blue walls, and a grey carpet lit by the steady glow of a fluorescent tube in a reflective holder directly above me.

A plump Caucasian woman wearing a plain navy-blue suit with a white and blue striped button-down shirt sat in the kind of blue plastic stackable chair common in the school rooms I grew up in.

The kind with the nice comfortable curve that hugs your butt, no matter how big it was.

Which was lucky for her.

Her identification card hung on a bright blue lanyard around her neck, but the glare of the light prevented me from reading it.

She sat directly across the scarred "beech" laminated office table from me, her head tilted back, looking up at the polystyrene soundproofing tiles on the ceiling.

Her blonde hair was pulled back in a long pony-tail, with a curled fringe like Sandy Olssen's in *Grease*. Upon whom it looked charming, but not so much for the woman.

There was some kind of Christmas song I vaguely recognised piped into the room, and she was humming along.

I was slouched in another blue plastic chair, wondering whether to tell her that her green apple scented body wash was too distinctive.

People would notice it, and therefore her.

Because she was my friend.

But, I knew she'd counter with the idea they would check her out as the source of the aroma, and promptly dismiss her.

Two half-empty white plastic cups of lukewarm dispenser water sat on the table between us.

Through a window on one side, I could see an office with a half-arsed attempt at strings of Christ-mas decorations, but no people.

And through a screened window on the other, nothing but the hint of sunshine from outside.

I felt drowsy in the mysterious warmth of the room, though I knew I was on the sunny side of the building. I don't know how I knew that, but the knowledge sat in my mind like a stone.

My eyes were shut, so I couldn't see what I was wearing, but I'm fairly sure it was the same as the blonde woman.

The door opened, as did my eyes, and I saw two men walk in. One was a tall, thin, older Caucasian with greying hair.

The other was shorter and by comparison fatter. Intriguingly dark; I had the idea he was Nigerian or Sudanese or something, not American.

They were also wearing navy-blue suits.

I had the idea it was some kind of uniform.

The black guy stood to the side, and a little behind the woman I faced, and the other behind me.

"Thank God," she said sitting up, "I'm so tired of pretending to be her friend."

I tried to stand up to protest, but couldn't move.

The white guy put his hand on my shoulder in case I managed to move, which made me struggle harder, but no matter how hard I strained my muscles, I couldn't move.

"This won't take long," he said, "just a couple of shots."

And then something thin and sharp like a needle hit me in the back of my head and pain blossomed.

I was thinking; this is it; *I'm going to die. They're going to find my splayed body in a filthy alleyway somewhere dressed in some kind of weird Harajuku outfit minus my underpants.*

Because what better way to disguise the death of a mole or a whistle-blower, or whatever I was than as a sex crime.

And with the feel of the second needle in my head, I was gone.

《《 • 》》

I woke suddenly, bolting upright to touch the back of my head, even before I'd wiped the drool from my mouth or the sleep from my eyes.

Of course there was nothing to feel.

It was just an incredibly vivid dream.

Wasn't it?

"Chasing rabbits in your sleep again Vee?"

I looked towards the male owner of the voice.

Noting I was in a pod of four desks. Each person sat with their backs to the others, facing a bright blue partition wall just tall enough to shield us from people walking by.

Thanks to the size and scope of the lavish Christmas decorations strung across the ceiling above me, the hard-wearing, blue-grey geometrically patterned carpet, and the quiet hum of conversation and air-conditioning around me, I could tell we were in an office of some sort.

Though I had no idea where that was.

And, I had no idea who he was, though I was infinitely reassured by his casual outfit of jeans and sloganed t-shirt.

I guessed Vee meant me.

Valerie? Veronica? Vivienne?

I ran out of ideas at that point - the names just felt wrong.

I kept my face perfectly still, trying to not betray my confusion.

"You know, twitching and yelping?"

Had I had this dream before?

Did I make a habit of sleeping at my desk?

I wiped my mouth, then rubbed my eyes.

"Urrrgggghhh," I said.

"You've got to stop working half the night. Go home and get some proper sleep. Come back tomorrow when you're feeling fresher."

Sounded like a great idea, but there was one small hitch.

I didn't know where I lived.

My mouth started watering with that weird metallic taste.

"I'm going to be sick," I said.

He leapt to his feet and rushed me out a door I hadn't noticed and into the male toilets.

Past the urinals where some guy tried to protect his privacy and through to the cubicles.

I would have laughed if I hadn't had my teeth clenched shut, and my hands covering my mouth in case I didn't make it.

He slammed a cubicle door open as my stomach heaved and emptied of what looked like noodles.

Or maybe tapeworms.

Urk.

When it was over, he supported me back to the sinks, where I didn't recognise myself in the mirror.

Not like when you look like shit, but like when you meet someone you have never met before.

Stealing glances at myself, I rinsed my mouth, and splashed water on my face, scrubbing it with my hands, but I still didn't recognise the woman in the mirror.

Weird.

And unsettling.

In the last five minutes he'd been good to me, seeming to know and trust me, so I gambled I could trust him.

"I don't remember who I am," I said, watching his face in the mirror.

He met my eyes, and obviously saw something, because he didn't question my assertion, just put a reassuring hand on my shoulder.

"We need to get you to a hospital straight away."

He came with me, and I wondered if he was my husband. But I wasn't wearing rings.

Boyfriend maybe?

Best friend?

Boss?

Or just a concerned colleague doing the right thing.

While we waited, I checked the handbag he'd given me, starting with the purse.

According to my driver's licence, my name was Vada Paloma and I lived at 2A/22 Smith Street.

It sounded like a made-up name if ever there was one.

My business card told me I worked at Johnstone Industrial Consulting where I was a "consultant."

Whatever that was.

One credit card, one myki, one library and one Medicare card in my wallet along with one $50 note, two $20s, 2 $10s and a $5 neatly stacked facing the same way by order of value, lowest to highest.

No coins, receipts or other ephemera.

An A6 diary told me nothing because when I fanned the pages, there was nothing in it.

Well, not nothing exactly, tucked inside the clear front cover protector was a photo of me, the guy and two others, grinning and holding half-empty pint mugs toward the camera.

"Team Christmas dinner last year," the guy said, then pointed at each of the people said, "Jennifer,

Vada, Carl, and me. I'm Jed, your Team Leader." He nudged me with his shoulder, "and best friend."

"How long have I known you?"

"Ah, let's see. You started working here in about October last year."

"That's pretty quick work."

There was something not right about that, but I didn't know what it was.

Even though I was feeling a warm regard for him, I couldn't tell whether that was from his recent care or some memory coming through.

"Yeah, I guess," he said, "but you are everything I didn't know I needed."

Definitely not right. Was I the kind of person who would target him for some reason? Was it something to do that memory/dream?

I turned my attention to the Hello Kitty pen in the diary cover's pen holder.

It was a little worn in the kind of way that suggested I'd used it a lot and had replaced the ink cartridge at least once.

I held it incredulously in front of me - I couldn't believe I was a fan, but the guy... Jed, laughed.

"Secret Santa, from me."

Explained that then.

A set of earbuds, but no phone.

"Where's my phone?" I asked.

"Ah, we check them in each day because we're working on confidential data. We didn't stop at the security desk to pick them up."

And that was the one thing so far that made perfect sense - no company wants their secrets made public, and I was a little bit glad that something made sense.

One key on a generic plastic keyring, so it seemed I didn't have a car.

Sunglasses, umbrella, small Japanese style hand towel, tissues, antiseptic hand wipes, tinted lip balm. And that was it.

Apparently, I travelled light and regularly cleaned out my handbag.

Nothing that told me anything about who I was, aside from someone who wanted to be prepared for eventualities. And that was not suspicious at all...

I felt made up, like a bit character in some spy story with no background.

Jed stayed with me during endless rounds of tests and scans, and during the long hours while I waited for someone to see me.

The short answer was that basically, there was nothing medically wrong. Nothing to suggest *any* kind of brain trauma.

Every single neural and blood test smack dab in the middle of the normal range. The doctor on duty suggested I stop stressing about it, but didn't offer any concrete suggestions about how to do that, or recover my memories.

Unbelievable!

Didn't even keep me in overnight for observation.

Sent the bill to Medicare, and me out onto the street in the wee small hours.

"Can I take you home?" Jed asked.

The truth was I was terrified; both of having lost my memory and going home.

I was not at all sure I wanted him to see anything in my apartment that might reveal who I was, or me trying to make sense of it.

But what if something happened on the way?

And if he was my best friend, wouldn't he have already seen it?

I nodded.

«« • »»

My apartment was one of two on the second floor of a three-story building.

He took the key from my hand and unlocked the door for me. Something he did with an easy familiarity, as if taking me home was something he did frequently.

I walked in and looked around me. It was basically two halves, one a "public" space with combined kitchen, dining and lounge, and the other split into a bedroom and combined bathroom and laundry, each with a door through to the other room and each other.

It had all the kind of furniture you'd expect, but there were no signs of me in it.

No art, no personalisation, no mess.

"This looks like a hotel, where's my stuff?"

"It is a hotel. You said you came from interstate and weren't planning to bring your stuff over until you found a place."

I did not point out how full of holes that story was.

"You left your stuff at your place and let it out."

Okay, that was a little more plausible, but for fourteen months?

Who does that?

My doubt must have shown on my face, and he said, "you weren't sure you were going to stay, and things got away from you."

Now that did resonate, so perhaps there was a kernel of truth in there.

I couldn't help myself, I yawned.

"Look, it's been a big day, why don't you get some rest. Don't worry about work, just come in when you feel up to it."

I nodded.

He walked across the room and enveloped me in a hug, "you're going to be okay."

I allowed myself to feel comforted, but I was still afraid.

"Do you want me to stay?"

Yes! Yes please, I thought, but I said, "no, I'm sure I'll be okay."

He kissed my forehead, and I wondered about the strength of our relationship.

Whether we were a thing, or he was taking advantage of the situation.

Or maybe he was holding back.

"No need to follow me out," he said and left.

I walked to the window overlooking the street and watched him walk up to the tram stop.

He turned to wave at me, and I waved back, before getting undressed and falling into the bed.

«« • »»

The next morning, I woke early, mainly because I hadn't closed the curtains.

I got out of bed to shut them in the hope of going back to sleep, but once I'd gone room to room, I wasn't really sleepy anymore.

Nonetheless, I lay in bed, looking up at the white ceiling, thinking about the situation I had found myself in.

Common sense had returned during the night. There was no way I'd been injected with something to block my memory by blue-suited people.

That was the stuff of spy thrillers and science fiction, not real life.

I'd just been working too hard, and stressing too much about whatever project I was working on.

The sooner I got back to normal, the better.

So I got up, got dressed, and went to work.

After checking out how to get there.

I clocked Mitchell straight away, perhaps because he was so out of place in the queue to look in the Myer Christmas window amongst all the mothers and hyperactive children.

Too still, and too alone in his navy-blue suit.

I was walking to the office with takeout coffees for the team in the hope they would go easy on me as I recovered my memory.

I was focusing on not spilling them into the cardboard carrier or burning my hands, so I was half a block away before I realised he was the white guy from my dream, and half a block further before I dredged up his name.

A chill ran down my spine as I realised I was looking in the shop windows around me to see if he was following me.

And before I knew what I was doing, I'd cut through an alley and was backtracking my path to lose him.

It seemed I had done this before, so many times I didn't even need to think about it. From deep inside me came a voice that told me he was such a bloody amateur.

I was shaking by the time I got to work.

I sat at my desk, looking at my blank screen thinking through the implications.

There were two options:

1. I worked for or with the navy suits.
2. I had nothing to do with them.

Either way, it seemed the brain injections were intended to delete some or all of my memory.

Because I was undercover at Johnstone's, or because I'd quit working for the navy suits.

Whoever they were.

I asked my gut about the security acronyms; AFP, ABF, ACIC and AUSTRAC didn't ring any bells, neither did ASD, ACSC, ASIO or ASIS. Or even ADF, DIO, and DOD.

None of them felt right.

Which led me back to private industry. And for some reason, that felt worse.

It was all very confusing.

I didn't feel I could confide in Jed, or anyone else for that matter, because who would believe you if you said *I had a dream some guy was doing something awful to me, and then I saw him on the street and now I'm very afraid he and I are up to no good.*

But whether I was a willing participant or not, he'd definitely done something to me.

And then I thought about the blonde woman, she'd said she was tired of pretending to be my friend, and that suggested that whatever it was they were playing at...

We were playing...

Whatever it was they were playing at, it was directed at something nefarious.

So, had she befriended me before or after I arrived at Johnstone's?

Had she lured me to their offices under false pretences, and permitted them to do whatever it was to an innocentish bystander.

Had I been placed at Johnstone's or was I a legitimate employee?

I needed to know more.

I thought the easiest thing would be to investigate myself first.

So, I started with an internet search of my name, and there was absolutely nothing there. Didn't matter which search engine I used, there was nothing to see.

Now it *is* possible I valued my privacy.

And it is equally possible I was planning a career in politics, or a branch of the secret service, and therefore had no social media presence on any of the main channels.

Or that I didn't have any friends.

Or was in a witness protection program.

But it's also possible I was a Luddite.

Bearing in mind I was seemingly the kind of person who was content to leave all her worldly belongings somewhere else for fourteen months.

My driver's license recorded the hotel address, and had a good long expiry, suggesting I had transferred from another state. Or had only just got it.

There was nothing unusual about the license, but if I wanted to access my records, I'd have to fill out a form and send it with a fee I thought was extortionate to their records office.

The Medicare card also had a long expiry, and while I could access my records, I'd need to register and blah blah blah, it sounded like a convoluted process.

The library card had no information, but I supposed they would have records of my loans for however long I'd been a member. Though of course, I couldn't remember my password.

I even checked the drive of the computer I was using, but there were no personal files, and when I questioned that, Jennifer said personal files weren't permitted.

Which I kind of understood, and approved of, because we were dealing with confidential matters.

But which also meant I couldn't keep any notes about myself in the drive as it would be too risky.

Somehow, I got through the day.

I hurried "home" as fast as the peak hour traffic would allow. But on the way, as I sat in the tram, I could smell green apple.

The scent had faded during the day, but it was still detectable.

I looked up and around, partly to check where I was, and partly to check for that bitch Fiona.

If looks could kill...

Well, suffice it to say she'd be raspberry jam lining the tram walls.

However, it seemed that inner me was still cross with her about the "pretending to be her friend" crack.

And I was a little bit impressed with how coolly I saw through her, face impassive, watching her from the corner of my eye, managing not to make eye contact.

So, was she following me, or did she coincidentally live in the area?

She was behind me as I jumped off the tram, so I ducked into a newsagent and bought a notebook.

There was no sign of her when I got back out, but I saw her again as I neared the hotel.

I started to get a little concerned - did we live in the same building? How the hell was I going to manage that?

Once inside my apartment, I opened the windows and saw her lurking in the street.

Which raised a conundrum of sorts. Was I back to being her pretend friend?

I decided to wait for the time being, to see whether she approached me. If we were back together, it shouldn't take long for her to arrive.

I shook myself and poured a glass of wine, grateful I was the kind of person who kept a couple of bottles of wine in my house.

And then, using the memories of every spy movie I could remember seeing, I checked out the apartment; rummaging through all the cupboards and drawers, pulling them out from the walls and looking underneath them.

No unexplainable electronic devices. I didn't actually know what bugs would look like, but I took comfort that the inner me didn't raise any concerns about what she saw.

A small capsule of quality casual clothing. No navy suits.

A couple of fantasy books from the library.

A collection of takeout menus stacked in a rack in the kitchen.

Enough crockery and cutlery for two people, courtesy of the hotel. With enough basic cookware to cook, though it seemed I didn't do any of that.

The usual toiletries and make-up.

A bowl of coins and a couple of hundred in $50 notes, and $30 in $5.

I did not find any records of my previous life, or the current one for that matter.

No real estate agreements, bank statements, employment contract, nothing.

So weird - how could I not have a paper trail?

Nor was there a laptop, or tablet. Though maybe they'd been stolen and I just didn't know it.

There was just me and my phone.

I grabbed out my new notebook and Hello Kitty pen, and sat at the table, but paused, pen wavering over the paper.

Was the reason there was nothing personal in here because I knew I was being monitored?

Did I have a separate room, or maybe another apartment for my personal things?

I put the pen down and closed the book.

I turned the TV on for some noise, and as it was nearly news time, swapped to the couch, settling down with the phone.

I woke up on the floor with a blinding headache. I opened one eye and looked around me; it was dusk. I started freaking out thinking it was tomorrow.

Then patted the floor around me to find my phone and checked the time, which was difficult because I couldn't see properly.

I thought the wiggly, staticky, blurry numbers indicated the same day, about an hour later.

I relaxed a little.

For the lack of being able to think of any better way to ease the pain at that moment, I crawled across the floor to the bathroom, stood wobbling as I drank some water, splashed my face and rinsed a flannel in water as hot as I could take it, then dropped back down on the floor and lay with it on my forehead.

After a while, the flannel cooled, and I turned it over just in case the other side was warmer.

And a little after that, I managed to lever myself upright and stagger to the kitchen.

I was cold, so I pulled the blanket off the bed on my way through.

The TV was still on, seeming especially bright, and if it was trying to remind me of something.

Mesmerised, I dropped to the couch, pulled the blanket more tightly around my shoulders, and looked at it.

I wasn't watching the TV per se, but I could see/remember flashes that weren't there before.

Wearing a low-cut slinky dress, dancing with strangers.

Glimpses of navy suited people; not the ones in my first dream memory but others.

Some gorgeous boy who I knew, but couldn't remember.

I couldn't tell whether the new memories were this life or the one before.

Then I heard a Christmas song on the TV, over an ad for some kind of sale.

And it clicked into place.

Not my memory, unfortunately, but that some kind of Christmas song had triggered new/old memories.

Deductively, the song that had been playing that day with the needles.

Presumably, I'd heard it the day before when I'd forgotten who I was.

And probably again on the TV just then when I blacked out.

So, I'd answered one question I didn't know I had, and triggered a billion more.

Had I been conditioned, or was it coincidental?

If I'd been conditioned, was I supposed to lay low for a year? Had they chosen a Christmas song so I wouldn't be triggered until now?

Were the navy suits hanging around waiting for my memory to come back?

Circling back through to were they "good" people or not?

And whether I should call Jed.

And almost immediately back to not really having anyone I could trust or rely on, except myself.

So, what was the trigger, and could I hear it without losing consciousness?

The TV was one of the ones that record a buffer, so you can pause, rewind, and fast forward.

Go to the toilet anytime you wanted, not cross your legs and wait for an ad break.

I rewound it to about where I remembered it being, and then punched the play button.

And set my phone to record it too.

I skimmed through the game shows, then played the ads, and about 15 minutes later I saw the one.

I started to feel ill with heartburn and nausea. I couldn't seem to get enough air in my lungs.

Time seemed to slow down, and every syllable stabbed me in the head.

I felt dizzy.

So very tired.

I lay on the floor gasping, trying to find the remote to turn the TV off with my useless fingers that seemed to have grown to an enormous size.

But the worst thing of all, was that I didn't recognise the song.

Then I was floating in another sea of blackness

This time, I woke in a hospital, feeling thirsty and hungover.

But fortunately, a room to myself.

I was pretty sure it wasn't the same hospital Jed had taken me to before.

But it had the same kind of lino on the floor with the edges that curved a little way up the wall to form a seamless skirting board.

And the same kind of textured tiles on the ceiling, presumably to dampen the sound of moaning from the next room. And if that was the case, it wasn't what you might call effective.

In my case, there was a stain on the tiles right above my bed that looked a bit like a cherub if you narrowed your eyes and looked at it like one of those 3D puzzle drawings.

And of course, the smell of boiled cabbage and processed meat flavoured bread crumbs for dinner.

A plastic jug of water, along with a plastic glass with a straw in it sat on a rolling table that had been pushed to the side.

And beyond the water jug, through the window, treetops and the kind of glow you get from street lights, or those bright lights over sports grounds.

No way the gauge when I was.

Something heavy weighed on my hand, and when I looked, it was someone else's hand and their head as well.

It looked a bit like Jed.

I twitched, and he jolted awake, "what's going on?" he said.

I gave him a minute, and then he asked, "what's the time?"

"I could ask you the same, but I'll ask for water first."

He grunted as he stood up and staggered to the table to drag it over. Then poured some water into the glass and held it a little under my chin where I could reach the straw.

And filled it up three times until I wasn't thirsty anymore.

"Other end?" he asked.

And I realised I needed to pee.

He helped me up and out of the bed, holding the rickety drip pole, escorting me through the bathroom door.

"Need any help with..." he gestured at me, then the toilet, in an embarrassed kind of way.

For a moment I was tempted to say yes, just to see how he'd handle that, but I said no.

"I'll be just outside, so let me know when you're ready."

I sat there for a while, wondering how I'd got to the hospital.

Someone must have come in, but who, and how.

I cleaned myself up, then called out, "I'm on my way."

He opened the door and stepped in to pick up the drip pole and take me back to the bed.

He plumped up the pillows before helping me back in.

And after all that, I was exhausted.

"So, what is the time after all that," I asked.

"Around three am. Do you need anything?"

I thought about it for a little. A cup of tea was tempting, but I was more tired than desperate for tea, so I said no.

"Go back to sleep then," he said, "I'll be here when you wake up."

And even though I had questions circling my brain, I did just go back to sleep.

≪≪ • ≫≫

The next morning I was woken by one of those ruthlessly efficient nurses, and Jed was nowhere to be seen.

"Where's my friend?" I asked.

"What friend," she said, "there's no one here but you."

I wondered if I'd dreamt him, or if he'd really been there.

She took my observations, and that made me wonder why no one had done them before.

Unless I was so very deeply asleep I didn't notice.

Or in a coma.

Or...

I couldn't think why else I might not have noticed.

She bustled away, refusing to answer any questions, only saying "doctor will be here soon."

Someone came in with cold white bread toast and little packets of margarine and strawberry jam for breakfast.

But given I hadn't eaten anything for dinner, I was hungry enough to eat them and very tempted to ask for another serve.

To wash it down, reconstituted orange juice, and a cup of lukewarm water with a teabag, one packet of sugar, and one single-serve pod of preserved milk, unaccountably served refrigerated.

By no means the best breakfast ever.

And then I waited for someone to come.

For Jed, or the doctor, or someone else to relieve the tedium of being in a single room with nothing to read and no phone to stream a show or play a game on.

After about a thousand years, a doctor arrived, clean and fresh with a crisp shirt and tied under his lab coat. Smelling of soap and some kind of woodsy cologne.

I was suddenly conscious of how dishevelled I was.

He seemed familiar, and as he flashed a torch in my eyes, and poked my face, and took my blood pressure, I was trying to place him.

He started humming a Christmas song, and I started to feel ill.

When he smiled at that, I knew who he was - the third guy from that room. The Nigerian or Sudanese or whatever guy.

I tried to scoot up the bed away from him, but he grabbed my shoulders to stop me.

At least he stopped humming.

"How did you find me?"

"We knew at some point you'd wake up to yourself, so we've been monitoring hospital admissions."

That wasn't reassuring in the slightest, "is this your doing?"

He smiled slightly, "it is and it isn't."

"For god's sake, stop dancing around the issue and tell me."

"What do you remember?"

Obviously I wasn't going to *tell* him I remembered nothing; I countered, "are you even a doctor?"

"I am."

He looked closely at me, looking for I don't know what, then sighed.

"My name is Aminu. I work for Jinko Cult Deprogramming."

"Cult Deprogramming? What the..."

"You followed Gregory John James into the Arcane Workers, intending to bring him out, but—"

"The what?"

"The Arcane Workers, does that resonate with you?"

The thing was I had never heard of them, but it felt true, so after a pause, I nodded.

I didn't trust him...

Them...

Whatever, but at least I was getting some answers.

"The Arcane Workers is a self-help type of cult, mainly targeting unemployed people with books and seminars.

"But some are drawn into their intensive, live-in programmes where you're essentially working as slave labour."

A chill went down my spine as I thought about that gorgeous boy I couldn't remember, "I followed him into the live-in programme."

"That's right."

"So what happened to... James, did you say?"

"Ah, he didn't make it," Dr Aminu made a sad face.

"Didn't make it out of the group, or didn't survive?"

"I'm sorry."

I was aghast - how could they get away with something like that, "they *killed* him?"

"Not as such, more along the lines of overworking and underfeeding."

So, they "just" stood by and let him work himself to death. That was criminal enough for me.

"And what are you doing about it?"

"We are sharing the information we've been gathering with the responsible Police Forces."

"I see."

I tried to summon up more memories, something that might be useful, but I was drawing a blank.

Aminu waited, and eventually asked, "do you remember who I am," he asked.

"I remember you being there when whatever that was in my head happened, and if you're a doctor, was that strictly ethical?"

"Intensive acupuncture. We had installed certain blocks prior to sending you in, and were trying to remove them.

"Do you remember who you are?"

"No."

"The name we gave you is Vada Paloma, but the name you were born with is Lily Robertson."

Lily Robertson; I rolled the name around in my head, and it felt right.

I tried to remember Lily's life, and there was nothing much, just the taste of vanilla on my tongue. I shook my head.

"We were unable to remove the blocks, so we left you with the implanted memories we gave you when you infiltrated the Workers. Am I correct that you don't have access to those either?"

By this point, I thought I could probably trust him, so I said "yes."

"And would I be correct in thinking you would like to remember your previous life?"

"Yes."

"It won't be comfortable."

I barely hesitated, "I will stick it out for as long as it takes."

"I know you will. You weren't ready to let it go last time, but I think you might be now."

《《 • 》》

What followed was two weeks of agony at a luxurious private clinic.

That Christmas song piped into my room nonstop.

Blinding headaches.

Throwing up almost as soon as I'd eaten.

Fitful sleep.

Punctuated by a succession of acupuncture treatments and herbal tonics.

Saunas and massages more like going twenty rounds with a giant kickboxing spider wearing boxing gloves.

Starving, feverish, freezing.

Until I lay on the floor like something you'd wipe off your shoe.

But at least I remembered who I was, and why that level of secrecy was required.

Though I'm still not entirely sure I was one of the good guys.

《《 • 》》

I was lying in a deck chair taking the sun when Jed arrived, drowsy in the warm eucalyptus-scented sunshine.

Magpies warbling from the treetops.

I'm not entirely sure who was more surprised, me or him because I'd been hoping I wouldn't see him again.

I had no idea what to say to him.

After all, I'd lied to him, even if I hadn't been aware of it at the time.

He stood looking at me, which was making me uncomfortable, so I stood up to talk to him.

And it seemed he didn't know what to say either.

"How have you been?" I asked at the same time as he said, "you look different," and we both laughed.

"Let's go for a walk around the gardens," I said, "they're really lovely," thinking I'd need the benefit of the exercise to stimulate my brain.

We walked across the sun deck, down the stairs following the path around a corner, out of sight of the buildings, he asked, "are you okay now?"

"Ummm. If you mean do I have my memory back, then yes, but I'm not sure how I feel about that."

"Vee, I—"

"My name is Lily Robertson, not Vada Paloma."

He didn't say anything for a while, not until we'd walked around a garden bed full of unattractive purple azaleas, "Lily suits you much better."

We walked a little further and I decided to just spit it out.

"I worked for a cult deprogrammer, though as a career choice it holds very little appeal for me now.

"It seems I went a bit too far undercover, and couldn't get back."

We circled some kind of weird geometric sculpture and started returning to the buildings.

He didn't say anything.

"I'm sorry I lied to you."

Still he didn't say anything, so I started resigning myself to starting a third life somewhere else.

As we were about to climb the stairs, he paused and looked at me, searching my face. "I've been trying to imagine it, but I can't. It must have been hard for you," he said.

Which was pretty much the last thing I'd imagined he might say.

"I guess your training helps you to become the person you need to be to achieve your objective, and that I have no idea who you are."

I shrugged, I couldn't deny it. That was exactly what I had done to win him over.

"I wonder whether the "real" you might be a more interesting person."

I did not shrug again, though I wanted to. I just waited to hear what he said next.

"But you were an excellent analyst and Johnstone's is prepared to keep you on, if you're willing."

I scuffed the ground with a toe, "and you?"

"I don't know."

"I don't want to make you uncomfortable, so I will decline if you're unsure."

He looked at me again, and I resisted the temptation to pat the air around my head to see if I'd grown a second head.

"You've been such a big part of my life last year that I just can't imagine you not being there."

I held my breath.

"And I'm so curious about who you are."

His smile caught me by surprise, and I gave him one of mine.

"Shall we give it a try?"

"I'd like that?"

"So, we'll see you on Monday then. Let's say 9 am?"

"I wouldn't miss it for the world."

THE END

ABOUT THE AUTHOR

Alexandria Blaelock writes stories, some of them for *Ellery Queen's Mystery Magazine* and *Pulphouse Fiction Magazine.*

She's also written five self-help books applying business techniques to personal matters like getting dressed, cleaning house, and feeding your friends.

She lives in a forest because she enjoys birdsong, the scent of gum leaves and the sun on her face. When not telecommuting to parallel universes from her Melbourne based imagination, she watches K-dramas, talks to animals, and drinks Campari. At the same time.

Discover more at www.alexandriablaelock.com